Over the Ivy Wall

By Rosa Sophia

Sunshine Press
Martinsburg, West Virginia

Over the Ivy Wall
Copyright ©2015, Rosa Sophia
Edited by Zee Monodee

ISBN: 978-1-939978-61-5

Dedication
For Jacob, who is always in my heart.

Clara Pendleton is a prisoner in her home. Always searching for new places to hide from her uncle, whose drunken attention terrifies and confuses her, she finds a tiny clearing in the back of the property near a disintegrating section of the ivy-covered wall that surrounds the estate.

Gaven Bridge has been sent to Clearwater to live with his Uncle Daniel. Never fitting in, he doesn't believe he'll ever meet anyone who understands him. But when he goes out for a walk in the woods, he happens upon a young lady sleeping soundly on a patch of moss.

A deep bond is fostered between them, helping Clara find the courage to change her life. When she finally decides to climb over the ivy wall and out into the world, there is no going back. Will Clara escape her horrible past, or will it destroy the love she and Gaven share?

Chapter One

The familiar hole in the wall admitted her like a portal to another dimension, and she crept inside with every certainty she'd be safe from him. And even if he found her, he was too big a man to climb in and retrieve her.

The house was old, undergoing work carried out by the semi-skilled sub-contractors her uncle knew, so she'd found a convenient hole in the attic, hidden behind mounds of storage boxes and crates marked with labels like *Christmas Decorations* and *Family Photo Albums*.

In her old house, when she was very, very little, her mother had let her come up into the attic with her and sort through old clothes. The sun-bronzed brunette with her ample laugh lines had told her in a sing-song voice, "The higher up you go, sweet pea, the closer you are to Heaven." She'd been joking, of course, because the attic was a dusty mess—with nothing divine about it—but Clara took it to heart and remembered her mother's words as she hid from her uncle, her slender form curled up and pressed against the insulation and the hard wood where the slant of the roof met the narrow beams of the flooring.

This was her most recent hiding place, because Uncle Harris had found her last one—a corner of the old shed in the back of the property, where her grandfather had once kept chickens. She was grateful for the immensity of the Pendleton estate; there were plenty of hiding spots.

But she was beginning to think the time had come to stop hiding.

Otherwise, who would protect her cousin? He was touching *her*, too.

Something in the insulation scratched her palm as she crawled in her pajamas across each hard, unyielding beam, squashing the fear that the floor might give out and cause her to plummet into one of the bedrooms below. At the hole—really a half-broken piece of drywall—Clara peered outward, cringing as her knees dug into the wood. The attic wasn't a pleasant place to spend time, but it wasn't easy for Uncle Harris to navigate, being a large, muscular man, built like a stone wall. And if he ever discovered her hiding place, it would still be easier for him to wait for her reemergence rather than go in after her.

Nighttime had come. She'd clambered in just before sundown, when Uncle Harris came home. She hid from him a lot, but she usually saved her disappearing act for weekends, when she knew he'd be drinking. The bottle of Old Granddad always waited for him on the antique end table beside his tattered old recliner; Aunt Nan knew to make sure it was there by the time her husband got home.

Glancing around the corner of the hole, she saw only blackness and dark shadows she knew were dusty boxes. She heard a creaking board that made her startle as something moved toward her. She started to scramble backward before a hand wrapped around her forearm; all breath escaped her and she couldn't even scream, but then—

"Clara, Clara, it's only me!" a voice hissed.

She froze. "Tammy?"

"Yeah." The girl's voice emerged as a whisper, then she crouched down. "You okay?"

"I think—*ouch*."

"What?"

"I think I got a splinter."

Tammy's small hands grasped Clara's shoulders, helping to tug her out of the hole and into the rest of the wide attic, where a moonbeam speared through a triangular window and illuminated only a small corner of the humid space.

The two girls huddled together against the drywall that separated the majority of the attic from the narrow channel that met the slope of the roof. A heavy guilt sunk over Clara as she cuddled against her cousin, who was only a few months younger than her. The two of them often sat like this in a hiding place, sometimes for an hour or more, arms entwined, cool cheeks pressed together, listening to each other breathe. In this house, there wasn't much comfort to be had unless they found it in each other.

"Tammy?"

"Yeah?"

"U-u-uncle Harris—" She hated how her voice often emerged in stammering gasps when she grew anxious or scared.

"I was helping Mom clean the kitchen," Tammy said, anticipating Clara's question. "He stayed in the den."

"T-T-T-T-Tammy—" Clara gasped, cursing to herself. She wanted to say how sorry she was. That she should be looking after Tammy. Maybe that was why her parents had died; maybe she was supposed to be here to help her. That was the only way it made sense.

There had to be logic somewhere, order nested in chaos.

If there wasn't a meaning for her parents' death—and a reason she'd arrived in the household of her father's brother—then she was enduring this for nothing.

For nothing at all.

And that possibility in itself was worse than death.

Chapter Two

Twelve years ago
Okeechobee, Florida

"Clara, eat your dinner, please." Her mother leaned her head down so she could look straight into her eyes. "You haven't touched your asparagus."

"I don't like asparagus." Clara stuck out her tongue, squeezed her eyes shut, and made the *icky* face. The expression only seemed to exasperate her mother further.

Instead of responding in annoyance, Mommy speared a stick of asparagus on her fork and took a hard bite, then tossed her head back and moaned in delight. Daddy, sitting beside her, chuckled to himself and eyed her with a mischievousness Clara didn't quite understand. Mommy was a thin woman, with a few extra pounds around the middle. Whenever Clara pinched at Mommy's chubbiness, trying to tickle her, Mommy said she hadn't quite been able to get rid of the *baby fat*, whatever that was. Daddy joked he had baby fat, too, as he patted his stomach while sipping the *beer* he said Clara couldn't have because she wasn't old enough.

Clara ate her asparagus, but with much reluctance. Then she went to bed, curling up under the covers, too sleepy to read a book.

She was an only child, and her parents doted on her. She loved spending time with her father in the shed, where she played with his wrenches while he worked. But she also enjoyed spending time with her mother, who'd taught her how to sew until Clara pricked her finger and decided sewing wasn't for her.

Her mother had tiny laugh lines around her deep brown eyes—the same color as Clara's—and she usually combed her shoulder-length auburn hair back, securing it with a clip. She didn't wear much make-up, but Clara loved watching her apply soft pink lipstick in the morning. She giggled when Mommy pressed her lips together, making a kissing noise. Then she would turn to Clara, kissing her on the cheek and leaving a wet, pink spot behind.

Her father's short-cropped red hair fascinated her when she was little; she often asked why her hair was brown instead of red.

"Can I have red hair?" she would wonder aloud.

"No, darlin'." Her father would scoop her up into his arms, tickling her. "You ain't a ginger like me!"

The evening tickling giggle-fest would always end the same way—with Clara tucked under her blue blanket while her father read *Goodnight, Moon* aloud.

On a Sunday evening, she was sitting on the living room floor playing with her stuffed animals, having decided to stay inside. Two weeks before Christmas, it was unusually hot out.

Her father came inside, mopping a cloth across his brow. His t-shirt looked soaked.

"Daddy, is it rainin' out?" Clara positioned a stuffed fox near a stuffed cow and a panda bear. The fox was attacking the farm, and she was the farmer who had to protect her cow as well as a host of other animals. Some of the other creatures were invisible.

Her father plopped down on the sofa in front of her and huffed. "No, sweetie. This is sweat." He tugged at his t-shirt as if to illustrate the fact, then ran a hand through his hair just as her mother emerged from the back of the house clad in short pants, sandals, and a pink blouse.

"You are *not* sitting on my couch looking like *that.*" Her mother's voice was stern, her eyes narrowed.

Clara positioned the cow so it didn't know the fox was coming.

"Aw, come on, honey. It's fine."

"You've got grass and dirt on your pants, Braden."

Clara's father shook his head as he stood. "I can't always look as nice as I do when we're at school."

"I don't think they'd let you in looking like that, dear."

Her parents both worked in a school, but not the one Clara went to. They called it a *magnet* school, but Clara didn't know what that meant; she just knew other kids her age went there. She wished she could go to the school Mommy and Daddy taught at, and she often begged, but they insisted she couldn't, the school was *out of their district*, whatever that meant.

With great care, she placed the panda bear near the cow; the panda would protect the cow when the time came.

"Dinner's almost ready." Mommy was in the kitchen now, a sharp *clang, clang, clang* resounding as she banged a metal spoon on a pot.

The fox went after the cow, but the panda came to her rescue.

Then Clara toddled into the kitchen and stood by the table, listening to her parents talk as she prodded the silverware, watching as her father fixed each piece every time she moved them. It was a fun game.

"So, are we still going out to Wyoming for Christmas?" Daddy didn't seem too pleased about the idea. He stood under the air conditioning vent and said, "Ahh," as he closed his eyes.

"Yes." Mommy stirred the pot of pasta with chicken and alfredo, Clara's favorite. "Sorry. That's the way it is."

"Ugh. I don't want to go."

"I don't understand why. He's your brother. Why don't you want to see your brother? And Clara should spend time with her cousin. They're so close in age; they should be best friends." Mommy glanced over her shoulder, her lips spread wide in a grin. "Would you like to see Cousin Tammy?"

"Yes!" Clara exclaimed. "Yes, yes, yes!"

"That's not fair," Daddy grumbled, "using the little one against me." He washed his hands at the kitchen sink, then dried them on a towel. "You know I don't really get along with Harris."

"But you like Nan."

"I love Auntie Nan!" Clara chimed in. "Can we go, can we, can we?"

"Yes, my little sweet pea, we're going to Wyoming for Christmas. You'll get to see snow for the first time." Mommy was very close with Auntie Nan; they talked on the phone at least an hour or so every week. And Clara always got to yell "hello!" into the phone.

"All right. We'll go," Daddy acquiesced. "But I won't like it."

"You just hate snow. *That's* why you don't want to go. It's not about Harris."

"It *is* about Harris."

Clara reached up, standing on her tip-toes, and snagged a paper napkin. She unfolded it, examined it, and began folding it into a new shape.

Her father, still dirty from mowing the lawn, leaned against the kitchen counter and crossed his large muscular arms over his chest. Clara eyed the tattoo on his arm, the one she loved so much; it was her name and her mother's name written in cursive.

"I just don't like—" Her father paused as if worried Clara would overhear. "His *tendencies.*"

"Braden, he's been *dry* for twenty years. Give the man a break. He's been going to *meetings.*" She checked the oven to see if the garlic bread was done, then pulled the pan out and placed it on the stovetop.

"*Mmm,*" Clara said loudly.

Her father chuckled, ruffling her hair. "You know how I feel. I don't need to say in front of you-know-who. *Big ears* over here." He winked at Clara.

"I know, my dear." Mommy leaned over and kissed her husband on the cheek. "I don't blame you, but this is how things are. We're going to Wyoming for Christmas. Everyone else is going—Aunt Janie and all the cousins, too. And they never go anywhere."

"Aunt Janie!" Clara exclaimed. She loved Aunt Janie because the last time she'd seen her, at a family reunion, Janie had given her chocolate. She'd never forgotten that.

"Oh, boy. She's going to fill our little one full of sugar," Daddy remarked.

"Sugar!" Clara echoed.

"Dinner's ready. But do me a favor and shower, will you? You can't sit down and eat looking like that." Mommy, always a stickler for cleanliness, wrinkled her nose in distaste and shoved Daddy in the direction of the bathroom.

The family sat down to eat, and Clara was content. Everything was as it should be in the life of this six-year-old.

For now.

Chapter Three

Summer proved a sweet respite. Clara would walk out into the heat and close her eyes, pretending she was in Florida. It wasn't the place that made her reminiscent, but her parents. She missed them. And she remembered how much they'd loved the Sunshine State, how they'd worked so hard to escape the cold.

Aunt Nan said Clara's father felt strongly about improving the American education system, and her mother had been just as passionate about it. Braden and Lynette Pendleton worked tirelessly to spread their love of education, one child at a time. They never forgot Clara; because of their dutiful, loving attention, she could read and write better than anyone in her kindergarten class.

Public school. That was something she had little experience with. She hadn't been to a regular school since the age of six. Since that day. The day she'd lost them both.

Uncle Harris was *old money*, and he was a *politician*. That's what her father always said, but he'd spoken the words with disgust. Harris was the older brother, and he'd been close with their grandfather, who'd died leaving all his money to Harris. Braden didn't end up with much, and Clara suspected it had left her father feeling angry and abandoned. But supposedly,

Grandfather Pendleton wasn't easy to get along with. He was brilliant, or he wouldn't have been the founder and CEO of a company that manufactured computer chips.

Clara opened her eyes. Where she stood on the side of the house, clad in a baggy t-shirt and jeans, she was alone. The wide estate covered a number of acres. A man from Jackson Hole mowed the area around the dwelling regularly, and the rest of the estate amounted to a carefully tended blend of pure chaos—a mix of trees and shrubs, tangled brambles lining the old stone walls that surrounded the property. It was old, Clara knew this much; the house had been built by her Great-Grandfather Pendleton, and encompassed the remains of an old farmhouse on the far side of the property. Nothing remained except the foundation of a house, and the stone walls that had once been part of the farm had been turned into larger walls that separated the Pendleton property from the rest of the world.

During the summer, she could use the outdoors as an escape.

"Clar?"

She turned to find Aunt Nan looking out the kitchen window at her. The first thing she saw was her rosy cheeks and thin lips, then the graying brown hair that hung in curls over her forehead.

"Come in and help with dinner?" Nan called out when Clara didn't answer.

Without saying a word, she walked around the house to the wide front porch, then went inside.

"Auntie, I'm here."

"I just need you to peel those potatoes while I finish making this pie crust."

"Pie?" she mumbled.

"Yes, I thought I'd make a pie for when your uncle comes home. He's had a rough week. Thought I'd make his favorite."

The apples were already peeled and ready. Clara started in on the potatoes.

"What do you mean, a rough week?" She spoke softly, but inside she was reeling, a chill passing through her. When Uncle Harris had a rough week, it meant he'd drink and berate Clara and Tammy. Nan would usually shrink away like a mouse. Only three o' clock now—plenty of time to sneak out, at least until Uncle Harris passed out for the night. Tammy was in her room doing homeschooling work; if she knew her cousin, she'd stay locked in there as long as she could, or she'd hide in the attic when it got cooler.

"I'm not sure. He doesn't talk much about it." Nan pressed in the corners of the handmade pie dough with artful precision. "He hasn't talked about much since…I mean, in years."

"Mm-hm." Clara knew what she meant—her parents' death. Her uncle's subsequent breakdown was the beginning of everything.

Or maybe it was the end.

As Nan began slicing the peeled apples, she chattered away about the week's events. "And I finally fired that cleaning lady," she finished.

"Which cleaning lady?"

"I just told you. Weren't you listening? You remember her. I know you do." Nan stopped chopping long enough to scrutinize her niece. "She can't be much older than you, maybe younger. The way my back's been bothering me after I fell last year, I need some help around here."

Clara remembered that fall. She'd been asleep when it happened, her bedroom door locked. She always wondered if maybe it *hadn't* been a fall. Maybe it had been a *push*. But she didn't pry. It wasn't safe to ask questions.

"So, what happened? With the cleaning lady, I mean."

"You were reading on the back porch, don't you remember?" Nan frowned. "You must've heard me yelling at her."

Clara shook her head. She'd gotten so good at jumping out of her body whenever she wanted, it was amazing the things she missed.

"Well, your uncle wasn't home. I came back from shopping and found *her* with the shower on, in the tub, *stark naked*, scrubbing the tiles."

Clara squeezed her lips shut, snorted, and chuckled as she worked. "Really, Auntie? Boy, I wish I hadn't missed that."

"Well, you're better off not seeing it. The view I got—let's just say she was scrubbing toward the *bottom* of the shower wall."

"What'd you do?"

"What do you think I did? First, I shrieked, then I said, 'goddamn it, girl, put some clothes on!' And then *she* shrieked, and then we were *both* shrieking—you mean to tell me you didn't hear this?"

"No. Although..." Clara scrunched up her nose. "I thought I heard something, but I thought it was the radio." Aunt Nan often listened to the radio while she worked in the kitchen.

"Well." Nan shook her head. "I said, 'what the hell are you doing?' and she said, 'cleaning the tiles and the bathtub,' and she was covering herself with the curtain. And I said, 'cleaning like *that?*' and she said, 'this is how I always clean *my* bathtub.'"

Clara doubled over with laughter, her gut clenching until it hurt. She couldn't remember the last time she'd laughed so hard—or laughed at all. "Oh my God, really?"

"Honestly, I don't think it's that funny." Nan's tiny smile, causing rare laugh lines to form at the corners of her eyes, betrayed her amusement. "Okay, maybe it's a little funny." She paused what she was doing to hug Clara, and they chuckled together until they couldn't anymore. Clara enjoyed Nan's closeness, and the scent of the vanilla perfume she always wore, before she pulled back and continued peeling the potatoes.

For a long time, they both remained silent as they chopped and peeled.

Then Nan asked, "Where were you last night?"

"When?"

"When your uncle was looking for you. Tammy said she didn't know."

"I was…outside." Her special hiding spot in the attic would remain a secret as long as she could keep it that way.

"Well, you shouldn't hide from him." Her tone had an edge Clara noticed immediately. She wondered if it was fear. "You know how he can get when he's angry and he's had a long day."

Clara knew. Too well.

"What time will he be home?" she asked, hoping she sounded casual. A slight tremor in her voice must've caught Nan's attention; the older woman eyed her with curiosity, but dared not voice the questions surely plaguing her mind.

"Maybe in an hour or so."

"Oh." Clara finished peeling the potatoes, but this time, her movements were so harried she cut into her finger, slicing the skin so blood flowed in a steady stream over the last potato. "Ouch!"

"Oh, Clara." Nan grabbed a few paper towels and helped her niece wrap up her index finger, squeezing it gently. "You have to be careful," she chided.

"I know, I know, I—" Clara winced at the pain as she glanced toward the clock. It was nearly six. "That's okay, Auntie. I'm okay."

"Here." She rushed into the nearby bathroom to grab a band-aid. Once the wound was cleaned, she wrapped it with a bandage, patting Clara's hand. "There you are, dear."

For a brief moment, their eyes met, and Clara wondered if her aunt knew what was going on in her house. Under her roof. She wondered if she knew about her husband, his *tendencies*. She was afraid to ask.

"It's still so bright and beautiful outside," Nan intoned, the corners of her lips twitching. "Why don't you go out?"

"Yeah. I think I will." They stared at each other for a split second, but it was long enough to tell Clara one thing; her aunt knew something. Maybe she didn't know everything, but she knew *something*, and she was afraid. Maybe just as frightened as Clara.

She was telling her to hide.

It wasn't a suggestion she enjoy the weather, but an offhanded comment intended to send her running.

And so she did.

Chapter Four

Twelve years ago
Okeechobee, Florida

Her father slumped onto the mattress beside her, yawning. "What story do you want me to read to you?"

"*Goodnight Moon, Goodnight Moooooooon!*" Clara crooned.

A dimple formed in his ruddy cheek when he scrunched his lips to the side, inadvertently showing his displeasure. "I read you that story every night, sweetie. Why not *Frog and Toad?*" He licked his lips and bounced as if excited, but trying to hide it.

Her mother peeked around the corner into Clara's bedroom. "Braden, just because *you* love reading *Frog and Toad* all the time doesn't mean your daughter has to."

"I, I...I do *not!*" he retorted. "Lynette, I can't help it if I want to *expand* the child's mind, get her onto something else, *interested* in something else."

"*Frog and Toad?*" Lynette stepped inside, leaning against the doorjamb, while Clara watched, then began playing with two of her stuffed animals.

"Okay, okay." Braden appeared to deflate. "*I love Frog and Toad,*" he grumbled. "Clara, whatcha wanna read?"

"*Goodnight Moon!*" The stuffed animals flew through the air and across the room for emphasis.

"Jeez, okay, kid." Her father grinned. "Don't get your pajamas in a bunch."

"Braden," her mother scolded. She came and curled up next to Clara, tugging her little body into her arms. "Read us a story."

"Fine. Here goes." He eyed Clara pointedly. "I know you have this memorized, little girl, so don't jump ahead."

Lynette smacked her husband's arm playfully, then giggled beside her daughter.

Clara loved moments like this. Every day, she looked forward to story time, when her father would read to her and her mother would cuddle against her. Sometimes, Mommy read a book, but usually it was Daddy. He always made up different voices for different characters, and sounded funny. He often acted things out by jumping around the room and making faces. Clara would giggle until she was so tired she couldn't keep her eyes open anymore.

When the story was over, her eyes had closed. She sensed her mother kiss her on the forehead as she whispered, "Goodnight, sweet pea."

Then her father kissed her on the temple and added softly, "I love you, baby girl."

She was too exhausted to respond. She listened as they stepped quietly across the carpeted floor. There was a pause, and she knew they were watching her sleep. They always said she was the best thing in their lives, and Clara believed them wholeheartedly. She felt so safe and secure snuggled under her blue blanket.

She listened as they stepped out, leaving the door ajar behind them.

Clara slept, and dreamt.

The next day, Mommy packed her lunch and tucked it into her little lunchbox, which was adorned with the image of a smiling cartoon princess. She took her to school and kissed her, squeezing her hand.

"Be good, my little sweet pea."

"Bye, Mommy!" Clara raced off to be with her classmates.

The morning passed uneventfully. They worked on a craft, getting paint all over the newspaper Ms. Kelly had spread across the smooth, round tables. Clara was scolded for trying to paint freckle-faced Jimmy Framm, even though he said she could.

Just before lunchtime, her tummy grumbled. Some of the other kids were whining they were hungry, and the teacher assured them it was nearly time to eat.

Then something strange happened.

Clara glanced up toward the front of the room as the door opened and clicked shut. Mr. Price, the principal, had stepped in. He was wearing black slacks and shiny black shoes, and the sleeves of his button-up shirt were rolled to the elbows. He also had on one of his funny ties, and Clara was squinting to try to see what it was. Clean-shaven and handsome, with a full head of thick black hair, Mr. Price looked nothing like Daddy.

What was strange was that he didn't crack a joke or announce a loud, comical "*halllloooooo, kiddos!*" to the children as he usually did.

Instead, he gently touched Ms. Kelly on the arm, brushing his hand lightly against the sleeve of her pastel blue, collared blouse as he ushered her to the edge of the room.

Clara saw him press his hand on the top of her back as if expecting her to fall. He never touched Ms. Kelly like that.

He leaned close and said something so quietly no one else could hear. The laughter of the children overrode everything else, and Clara barely saw his lips move.

Then Ms. Kelly gasped, covering her mouth.

She glanced so briefly in Clara's direction it was almost imperceptible, before she dashed from the room with Mr. Price following closely behind.

As the door shut, Clara heard a loud sob from outside.

Something was wrong. Terribly wrong.

Chapter Five

Clara grabbed her notebook, stuffing it into a small bag with a few pens, her camera, and an extra long-sleeved shirt—just in case going out tonight meant staying in the bushes until after it got chilly. She never left the house unprepared. Not that she ever went beyond the walls of the estate.

She knocked gently on the door across from hers. "Tammy? Tammy, it's me."

The door opened a crack. Tammy peeked out as if to make sure, then opened the door wider to let her in. The two of them were physical opposites. While Clara was thin and curvy, with her mother's dark brown hair reaching to her shoulders, and pale blue eyes, her cousin Tammy was a bit chubbier, with light brown hair and eyes to match. She was pretty, but she hid it behind hair she didn't comb well. Because she always let her roguish bangs cover her face, her skin was pocked with zits, and she hung her head constantly, forcing her body to slouch. Like Clara, she wore baggy clothes.

Tammy shut the door behind Clara and locked it quickly, then both girls sat down on the twin canopy bed. Her room looked pretty much the same as it had twelve years ago when Clara had first arrived—an overabundance of pink, with posters of boy bands adorning the walls, music that Tammy never actually listened to. She had an old portable CD player, and she would lay on her bed for hours playing the same albums over and over—Bach, Stravinsky.

Something about the room, the decorations, betrayed Tammy's mental absence, her stunted growth. Like Clara, she had perfected *jumping*, which was what both girls termed their shared ability to leave their bodies whenever they needed to. Whenever something *bad* happened.

The jumping meant she wasn't around much, and so this room was just where she kept her body. Her mind roamed elsewhere.

"Tammy, I'm going outside. Wanna come?"

Tammy shrugged, already slumping forward. She tugged her headphones off, letting them dangle around her neck. Clara could hear the strong tones of a pianist, then the lilting notes of a violin streaming from the earpieces.

"Not really," she mumbled. Then she glanced up, looking excited. "I'm halfway through *Twenty Thousand Leagues Under the Sea*. It's the best book ever!"

"Shouldn't you be reading some mushy story about boys?" Clara joked.

"What boys? I never see any. Unless you count when I go to the grocery store with Mom."

"At least she *lets* you go to the grocery store. She won't let me out of the house."

"You came with us to the mall last month."

"*Whoop-de-do-da*. I hadn't been outside the front gate in two years." Clara smirked. "That was pretty cool, though, the way that guy winked at me. I thought I would die!"

"He was cute." The dimples in Tammy's cheeks deepened. "I think he liked you." Then her expression fell. "You're so pretty. I'll always be ugly and stupid." She clenched her paperback Jules Verne so tightly, Clara thought the binding might snap.

"What are you talking about?" She gently brushed the hair away from Tammy's eyes, tucking it behind her ears. "You *are* pretty. You just don't know it."

"I guess I'm glad I'm not sexy like you." Tammy's face scrunched up so she looked like a pinched orange. "Maybe that's why—I mean, *never mind.*"

They both fell silent.

"Uncle Harris sure was pissed when we came back from the mall," Clara mumbled after a while.

"I know. He screamed at Mom. I hate it when he does that. He said he wouldn't let anything happen to you, like what happened to your...*well.* Uncle Braden and Aunt Lynette."

Again, they were silent. Then Clara whispered, almost inaudibly, "I'm always afraid I'll forget what they sound like, what they look like."

Tammy squeezed her hand, pulling it into her lap. "You won't forget. I know you won't."

They sat there for a moment longer until Clara realized the time. It was getting late; Uncle Harris would be home soon.

She stood hurriedly and threw the strap of her bag over her shoulder. "Wanna come? Come with me, please." She tugged on her hand, almost begging.

Tammy looked up, her eyes moist as if she might cry. Just as quickly, the expression was gone and she smiled warmly, waving her cousin away.

"Nah, I really don't feel like it. You go on ahead. I have to find out what happens." She lifted her book, then flopped back on her bed. "Love you, cuz."

"Love you, too, Tammy."

She glanced back at her before shutting the door, knowing Tammy would jump up immediately to lock it. She left her there with her Jules Verne and her Stravinsky, before running down the hall, down the steps, and out of the house—unable to squelch the growing sensation that she was betraying her cousin somehow.

She saw him parking his red pick-up truck just as she darted toward the back of the house. He called out, "Clara, where're you headed?" He sounded jovial enough, but she wasn't buying it. He was never happy, especially not when Aunt Nan said he was having a *rough week*.

He followed her around the side of the house; she could hear his footfalls. He was a big man, and didn't go unnoticed. There wasn't much to the gardens, which Nan had once kept up herself until she hurt her back. Now a gardener came twice a week to look after the back yard, where rocks mapped out circular beds and little walking paths weaved around reflective ornaments and a few inquisitive-looking lawn gnomes.

Beyond that stretched a patch of wilderness and huge bushes that flowered during the spring and summer months. She'd seen animal paths through there, but would she fit? She panicked.

With only seconds to decide, she dove into the underbrush, throwing her jeaned knees onto the dirt, leaves, and twigs. She could at least tuck herself in here until he left, then figure out where else to go. She shoved her body in as far as she could, until she knew she couldn't be seen.

Then she froze, knowing he was out there.

Surveying the shrubs.

Looking for her.

"Clara, where'd you scamper off to? It's nearly dinnertime. Your Aunt Nan will be wondering where you went."

She slowly shifted, careful not to make a sound. Through the dense foliage, she made out a corner of one of his shoes, then a flash of brown she was sure must be his slacks.

Maybe he'd given up. Or maybe he guessed she'd gone back inside. Regardless of the reason, it seemed as if he'd left a moment later. She didn't want to check, frightened he waited for her out there.

She sat for a while as the sun began to set, and it grew darker faster inside the bushes. She brushed a spider off her arm, tugged her bag against her chest. She looked to her left and right, trying to decide what to do next. This path must've been made by raccoons or some other night creatures. It continued on, seeming to widen. Curiosity begged her to investigate.

Clara loved small spaces, and nature fascinated her. Plus, probing the shrubs meant she'd have more precious time alone. She held her bag against her and crawled forward, reaching up every so often to pull her hair away from twigs and branches. The path widened until the bushes opened up, giving her entrance to a small clearing where moss covered the ground, reaching out to kiss the stone wall surrounding the property. Here she was, at the edge of the Pendleton estate, away from view in a world of her own. She liked it here.

Conveniently, a portion of the wall wasn't covered with poison ivy, so she leaned back here and stretched her legs. The clearing appeared sizable and comfortable, a surprising find. A new hiding place she quickly earmarked in her mind. She spent a few minutes tugging the leaves and twigs out of her hair and brushing off her jeans. It'd begun to get chilly, so she pulled on the long-sleeved shirt she'd tucked into her bag. It was soft and warm, perfect for this weather.

She set her back on the ground before standing. Stretching onto her tiptoes, she peered over the shrubs and saw the top of the house. She hadn't realized it, but she'd gone down a slight hill as she'd crawled, meaning her hiding spot was even more concealed than she'd thought.

Perfect.

She wasn't concerned with the growing dark; she had a flashlight and bug spray in her bag. The Girl Scouts could've learned a thing or two from Clara Pendleton.

The clearing allowed her ten feet or so to move around, and it was covered with that soft moss that made it feel as though she walked on air. She investigated, stepping along the edge of the wall, careful not to touch the poison ivy. Another kind of ivy, which she knew instinctively was *not* poisonous, also decorated the disintegrating stone wall.

Around the rest of the property, the wall was kept up, but here, where it proved difficult to reach, it had begun to fall apart. Clara always knew the wall to be as tall as she was, but here, it was broken and dipped down so it reached up only about three feet high in one spot. Peering beyond that, she saw a deer path and thick trees and foliage, a beautiful forest teeming with life.

For now, she would stay where she was. Content, and feeling safe for the first time in a while, Clara stretched out on the moss and rested her head against her bag, using it as a pillow. There weren't very many bugs, and the slightly chilly summer evening lulled her to rest.

Soon, she drifted to sleep, listening to the crickets and cicadas as they sang their syncopated lullabies.

Chapter Six

It was just after five-thirty when Gaven decided to go for a walk. In this strange new place, his routine was obliterated. In West Palm Beach, he had a *method* for Friday nights. He went to City Place; sometimes he walked Clematis Street. He would go into a bar and order the cheapest beer on the menu, then stand there wondering how to strike up a conversation with one of the women in attendance.

But none of them seemed to notice him. And they were all immersed in their own egocentric worlds. They wore tight clothes and displayed their bosoms and smooth thighs as though they were selling something. Gaven enjoyed the view, but the sounds of their voices—their tinny laughter and propensity to use *like* between every other word—grated on his nerves.

Being twenty-one wasn't so wonderful. It meant he could go into bars, not that it mattered; he'd been drinking since the age of fourteen when his neighbor started buying him beer. He discovered it turned him into someone else, someone he could handle. The Gaven who drank could talk to people. He could strike up a conversation and stand there pretending to be like everyone else, even though he was so different it sometimes made him want to scream. Or die. Or both. The emotions proved just out of reach. The drugs, the mood stabilizers, saw to that. He hadn't been himself for a year and three days; he was counting.

His mother had brought him to a psychiatrist who told him he needed the medication. Now, Gaven had difficulty feeling anything at all.

So when the blond jock had bumped into him two weeks ago, nearly spilling Gaven's beer, he'd barely reacted. He'd just looked at the beer sloshing in his cup, then up at the young man in his brand-name polo shirt and designer jeans.

The sneer on the man's lips made him back up a step, and the blond shouted over the blaring music, "You stupid mother-fucker, you got my shirt wet!" Clearly, the man was drunk, and Gaven was not. He hadn't gotten his shirt wet, either. He started to say as much, but the jock cut him off. "You wanna fight, you piece of shit?"

"No." Even if he'd wanted to, Gaven couldn't get angry anymore. He wished he could. He remembered how much he'd *wanted* the ability to be furious, but it wasn't coming. It wasn't there. It was impossible.

The jock wouldn't leave him alone, even when he'd tried to walk away. He left the bar, and the guy came after him, goading him. His friends followed. And when the blond threw the first punch, Gaven *still* couldn't get mad enough to retaliate. But in a situation like that, he did what he had to do to protect himself.

Without anger, without a shred of remorse, without any emotion whatsoever, Gaven had used unadulterated logic to lift his fist and plant it squarely into the man's face.

And that, indirectly, was what brought him to Clearwater, Wyoming.

His mother had been trying to *help him* since he was a little boy, but he knew better; she was trying to change him. He'd become practiced at the art of discerning the meaning in expressions, body language, and all the little things people did to betray their true motives. He always said he could figure a person out in thirty minutes or less. And he was always right. *Always.*

When Mom sent him to live with his uncle after he'd broken the jock's nose, he was somewhat perturbed she'd found a way to get rid of him, and content he'd finally gotten out of West Palm Beach, where it seemed like everyone he met presented a fake persona, a thin veil of mock personality that dissolved as soon as he looked into their eyes.

Uncle Daniel seemed a little different.

His messy brown hair contrasted with his deep blue eyes, and he smiled a lot; the teasing lines around his eyes and mouth proved it. Uncle Daniel and Gaven's mother, Rose, had grown up in Georgia, both retaining the country twang that made them approachable and projected a sense of ease—to most, anyway. He never felt the comfort from his mother, but he sensed it in Daniel. The man was as transparent as the beer glasses he rubbed clean in the bar he owned.

Damn. If only he'd let me have free beer.

Daniel lived above the bar, and at night, the blue neon sign that read *On the Rocks* in cursive lettering illuminated the living room with an unnatural glow. Gaven was glad he had his own room, that he didn't have to sleep on the couch. With the bright blue light invading his retinas, he'd never be able to rest.

His uncle was nice enough, giving him privacy and freedom despite what Gaven's mother ordered. "Just remember to take your pills on time," Daniel had advised. "Other than that, you can do whatever you want. There ain't much to do around here, anyway, I'll admit. Just be careful and keep your head on your shoulders, kid." Gaven took the back stairs two at a time, emerging into the hall in the back of the bar. From there, he turned the old knob of the heavy wooden door and stepped out into a small parking lot behind the building. His uncle was at work in the bar and wouldn't even know he'd left.

He walked around the establishment and out toward the road, glancing back to see a laughing couple enter the building as the sound of Bob Segar's voice flowed into the street. When the door shut, the music grew muffled, and Gaven walked down the sidewalk with his hands in his pockets.

The town was the total opposite of what he was used to. West Palm Beach had been flat, every street lined with palm trees, and nearly every road had multiple lanes. When he'd still had a car—before he wrecked it in an accident that *wasn't* his fault—driving in West Palm had been problematic, at best. In this tiny town of less than five hundred people, Gaven doubted driving was a big deal.

As he walked down Queen Street, where the bar was located, he spotted a few ladies congregating in front of Fast Check Grocery. They glanced his way as if gossiping about the newcomer, then quickly averted their gazes.

What is this, Maberry?

He quickened his step, taking in the brick buildings, old-style architecture, and snow-topped mountains that rose all around him, surrounding the town as if to separate it from the rest of the world.

He felt out of place here, but he just had to find something to do. Anything.

Maybe he couldn't feel much, but he wanted to discover something. Reading, learning, exploring; that's what he most adored. No matter the town, no matter how small or large, there was always something new to learn. And whatever it was, he'd find it—just like he always did.

Chapter Seven

Main Street ended.

And like a tourist turning in circles at the end of Clematis Street, Gaven wondered what to do next. He spent some time looking in store windows, noticing it was getting late. He didn't buy anything; his mother would keep sending him money until he got a job, but his cash flow was limited. A knoll at the edge of the street and a paved drive led up to Winterbloom Bed and Breakfast. A quaint painted sign announced its presence, and the leafy green oaks flanked the asphalt in a welcoming manner.

The road continued out of town, and there were some houses, a few long roads branching out, and some farms farther away. He walked until the sidewalk ended, then wandered past Winterbloom. A few cars drove by, and an old truck heavy with hay.

The woods beckoned to him, and he answered the call.

Though he'd grown up in the city, he relished a trip to the countryside, and enjoyed the sprawling fields where cattle grazed in Florida around Lake Okeechobee. He'd explored the area in depth, and found the atmosphere calming. He hoped to find a similar calm in the woods around Clearwater.

He remembered when his mother took him to the Everglades, and they'd visited Everglades City. They'd stayed in a little bed and breakfast, then ridden on a swamp buggy the next day. Though Gaven had been twelve years old at the time, he hadn't forgotten his fascination with the trees that rose out of the marsh, and the mock Indian village someone had set up to represent how the Seminoles had once lived in the hammocks. What was it like, living in these cold mountains, as opposed to the humid stickiness of South Florida? He'd only been here two weeks, which wasn't enough time to tell.

Farther down the road, he found another long driveway—Winterbloom's neighbor. Gaven forged a path between the two, heading for the woods, operating on the principle that if you did something fast enough, people didn't notice you.

When he reached the edge of the woods, he blazed a trail through a few shrubs, discovering a deer path that led between the trees. It was tranquil here; Gaven had always been more comfortable in nature. He loved animals, but disliked people. People *were* animals, but they always had an agenda, some diabolical purpose. He didn't trust the majority of the people he met; they were savages wearing society's imposed mask, the façade of the civilized. Animals, on the other hand, had not been tamed by society. They acted on impulse, but a deer wasn't apt to kill another deer. Humans killed humans. Animals didn't plot against each other, insult, or jeer; they just did what animals did best—they subsisted.

As he walked away from Clearwater, between the trees and across the underbrush, he could hear the hum of a highway far in the distance. He slapped at an insect on his arm, then stepped over a patch of poison ivy.

He followed the narrow deer trail, which didn't stay straight, but wound until it seemed like he'd walked in a circle. Because of the occasional obstacles, the short walk took a long time.

And when he reached the stone wall, he figured he'd traveled about a mile, maybe less, away from the tree line. The wall looked old, like it'd been part of a farm one day long ago. It was covered in a couple different types of ivy—poison ivy included. He'd learned about the awful, itch-inducing plant when he'd visited Fisheating Creek near Lake Okeechobee and returned home with a terrible bumpy rash.

Glancing to his right and left, he saw the wall continued in both directions. He wondered how far it extended, but he wouldn't find out tonight. It was beginning to get dark.

He turned, ready to walk back the way he'd come, when his ears perked up. He was certain he'd heard a soft mumble, maybe a groan.

That's when he leaned over the broken part of the wall, and saw her curled up in the moss. A girl, with hair the color of tree bark splayed in a mess around her narrow face, her arms wrapped around her bosom as if to fight off the growing evening chill.

When she opened her eyes, she saw him and shrieked, then slapped a hand over her mouth in sheer terror.

Shit. Good job, Gaven Bridge. You've done it again.

Chapter Eight

When she yelled in surprise, fear surging through her veins, she realized Uncle Harris might hear her. Which was worse—having him discover her new hiding place, or being caught unawares by a strange man?

"I'm sorry." The young man tucked his hands into his pockets and backed away as Clara rose to her feet. "I really, really didn't know anyone was there. I'll leave you be."

His apology seemed sincere, but his tone was flat, his deep brown eyes mistrustful—of what, she wasn't certain.

"Wait. Who are you?"

He stopped, seeming unsure as to whether he should answer her or not. Finally, he said, "Gaven Bridge. I just moved here." He forced a chuckle, a sound that wasn't at all natural; it was as if he'd practiced it over and over, trying to make it right but never quite succeeding. "I'm sure you know everybody around here. This town is much smaller than what I'm used to."

Clara frowned, relaxing as she tucked her hands into the pockets of her jeans, mimicking his uncomfortable stance. "Actually, I don't know anyone around here. I don't get out much."

"Oh. Well, what's your name?" His tone was clipped, harried. Again, as if he'd studied dialogue in books, but couldn't quite get a handle on social interaction.

"I'm Clara Pendleton." She bit at her bottom lip, then added, "What are you doing all the way out here? In the woods, I mean."

"Just walking. I don't like being around people. I like the woods."

"That's funny." Her lips quirked upward. "I wish I could be around people more."

"Why's that?" He took a few steps forward.

"I never get out of this place." She gestured behind her. "I just found this little spot." She fidgeted where she stood. "Why am I telling you this? You're a total stranger."

"You must trust me, then." When he took another step forward, only the disintegrating wall separated them.

"I guess so." She breathed a sigh of relief, experiencing a sense of ease around him. She wasn't sure what it was; maybe she just hadn't been around other people in so long, it felt refreshing to talk to someone.

"Can I ask you something?"

"Sure," she replied.

"Why were you sleeping out here?" He glanced up at the sky. "It's getting dark. Shouldn't you be at your house? And, why did you say you never get out? What did you mean by that?"

She smirked, watching the way the breeze tousled his smooth, fine brown hair. "That wasn't just one question, that was a lot."

"I didn't say I would ask one question. I said *can I ask you something*, which could be anything, and *doesn't* clarify how many questions I'd be asking. So, I can ask as many as I like."

"Well!" she huffed. "Point taken. Let's see. I was sleeping out here because it's a lovely evening and I'm tired. The moss is really soft and makes a nice bed. As for the house, yes, I guess I should be there. But I don't want to be. To answer your last question, when I said I never get out, I meant *I never get out*. It's a long story. But I've only left this estate a few times since I got here when I was six. *Again*, why am I telling this to a total stranger?"

"You trust me, remember?"

They stood only a few feet apart, and when he spoke, Clara could see the imperfections in his teeth; a few in the front row were crooked. When he smiled, a dimple formed only in his right cheek, and his eyes were so deep she found herself staring into them.

He seemed to be assessing her, as if trying to figure her out. He shook his head, frowning. "This will require further study," he said, hopping up to sit on a portion of the wall that didn't have poison ivy.

"What will?" she asked, leaning against the brick.

"You. You're different than the others."

"Other…?"

"Other women."

"Oh. I haven't met many of those, either."

"You're younger than you appear." He raised an eyebrow. "You have more wisdom than you should at your age. You know too much."

"How did you…?"

"I can figure people out," he explained. "How old are you?"

"Seventeen. I'll be eighteen in a couple weeks. How old are you?"

"That is irrelevant." His lips twitched upward, and the dimple appeared.

"How old are you, Gaven?" She narrowed her eyes, crossing her arms over her chest. "Tell me, or I won't talk to you anymore. My aunt always told me never to talk to strange men."

"I'm twenty-one."

"Then I guess I shouldn't flirt with you anymore."

"Were you flirting?"

He appeared so stoic, leaning there against the stone, she couldn't help but goad him. It occurred to her that despite how quickly she'd been forced to grow up, she was still a seventeen-year-old girl at heart. She smirked. "I don't know. Maybe."

"You don't live here with your parents." Gaven nodded toward the estate.

"How'd you guess that?"

"I listen closely to what people say. I pick up on their mannerisms." He cocked his head. "You intrigue me because I'm still trying to figure you out."

"And once you figure me out, what then?"

"I think I'll still be intrigued."

"Ah, I see. Well, to pique your curiosity, I live here with my aunt and uncle. My uncle is my father's brother."

"What happened to your parents?"

Clara froze. When she was six, she'd come to live here, but Uncle Harris and Aunt Nan had kept her away from the rest of the world. *No one* had ever asked her that question. She'd never had to explain it. A chill passed through her and she fought the urge to cry.

"I…I r-r-really should go. It's g-g-g-getting late." Dusk had fallen; she tugged her flashlight out of her bag. With any luck, Uncle Harris would be asleep in his easy-chair by now, and she could sneak past him and up the stairs.

Gaven frowned. "You're stuttering. Is something wrong?"

"No, I'm f-f-f-fine. I j-j-just have to go." She squeezed the words out, wincing. Sometimes it was so hard to talk. "You'd better hurry back, or…you m-m-might get l-l-lost."

"Can I see you here again?"

"Sure, I…I guess so. Um, I'll be here t-t-tomorrow," she added without thinking. Tomorrow being Saturday, Uncle Harris would be home. She'd definitely want to stay out of his path. Maybe it would be nice to have company.

"Okay." And with that, he turned and walked away into the darkness.

Clara found the passage through the shrubs, got down on her hands and knees, and crawled back toward the house with the flashlight gleaming in her hand, still trying to figure out what had just happened—and why.

Chapter Nine

The gleam of the flashlight led her through the underbrush, and by the time she emerged, her jeans were stained green and brown from dirt and grass. The moon hung in the sky, and she switched off her flashlight, not wanting to be seen from the house. Her heart hammered in her chest as she shouldered her bag and crept through the yard, ducking past the yellow light that splashed across the grass from the upstairs window—her aunt and uncle's bedroom.

The house was vast, having been built many years ago. She would've guessed the 1800s, but she had no idea when the area was settled. Her interest in Clearwater, in this house, in Wyoming in general, amounted to *nil*. How could she be interested in a town she'd never been permitted to explore?

When her parents were killed, it planted the seed of unrest in Uncle Harris, and exposed him for the control freak he was. He pulled Tammy out of school, and wouldn't let Clara attend. He said there were monsters out there, that it wasn't safe.

What a fucking hypocrite, she thought as she tried to rub the dirt from her jeans. She knew Aunt Nan would scold her if she saw this; the pants were fairly new.

She wandered around the huge house and through the side garden, thinking. What made Uncle Harris view those in the outside world as monsters, when he was no better? She wondered what he saw when he looked in the mirror.

Creeping around the side of the house and up to the front, Clara saw the living room windows were darkened. This would be her chance. She tried the knob on the kitchen door—not locked. Aunt Nan knew she'd gone outside, and she'd left it open for her.

Thank God.

Now Clara hoped luck would continue to favor her as she made her way upstairs.

The kitchen stretched out huge, imposing in the dark. It had once been half the size, but the wall that separated this room from the summer kitchen, where an old stove took up a dark corner, looking very much like a pot-bellied, grimacing man in the eerie dim light of the moon, had been removed. The whole room had been modernized a few years back, under the insistence of Aunt Nan. Uncle Harris had acquiesced because he was a sucker for her cooking, the only thing that could tame him.

Clara made her way through the shadows, which seemed hauntingly alive. She removed her sneakers, then scooped them up, before stepping soundlessly onto the smooth wood floors that extended into the dining room and the huge living room on the other side, where wide, curtained windows surrounded a large couch, loveseat, and Uncle Harris's favorite worn recliner. The moonlight reflected off the flat screen television, making her heart jump. She'd almost thought it was a person.

Finding the carpeted staircase, she took her time, stepping carefully because she knew where every weak spot was. She avoided the areas that *creaked* and *squeaked*, breathing a soft sigh of relief when she reached the top without incident.

The soft light extending toward her made her flesh crawl with terror—until she saw Tammy's wide eyes.

She hurried to her cousin's bedroom, and Tammy ushered her in, shutting the door behind her as quietly as she could.

"You're back," Tammy whispered.

"Yeah. It's not that late. Why are they in bed already?" Clara gestured toward her aunt and uncle's bedroom.

"They're not really. Well, Dad didn't feel good. His stomach is bothering him again, and he's been getting dizzy."

"I read about those stomach pains in the library," Clara said, referring to the enormous room on the third floor that Uncle Harris's grandfather, then his father, then Uncle Harris himself, had lined with books.

"What do you mean?" Tammy asked, sinking onto her mattress in her pink flannel pajamas. The window was open, letting in a cool breeze.

Clara shook her head. "Sclerosis of the liver. It happens when you drink too much."

"Mommy said he was clean until just after your parents died. Then, *bam*. He quit going to meetings and started drinkin' again."

They heard the door to the bedroom down the hall open and shut, then Aunt Nan's familiar footsteps shuffling along the carpeted hall and toward the stairs.

"She'll probably read for a little while. She won't get you in trouble." Tammy curled up with a big fluffy teddy bear she'd gotten for her birthday. "You might get in trouble for your clothes, though. You look like you've been rolling around in the dirt."

"I kinda have. Do you have an extra pair of PJs?"

"In the bottom drawer of the dresser."

Clara dug around until she found a pastel blue pair with cartoon ducks all over them. Their silly smiles lightened her heart, and she quickly tugged off her jeans and shirt, pulling on the soft pajamas before she jumped onto the bed with her cousin.

"Where were you, anyway? You didn't find another hiding place, did you?"

Clara tugged herself across the mattress and over to Tammy, cuddling up against her. They both tucked their heads against the feather pillows. The soft glow from three nightlights bathed them in a comforting light.

"I *did* find another hiding place," she whispered. She told Tammy about the little path through the bushes.

"The attic sounds easier. But at least when you're outside, you're farther away from Daddy."

"I guess there are good things and bad things about it. But..."

"But what?"

"I met someone out there."

"Huh?" Tammy's cute little nose scrunched up as she assessed her cousin, giving her a look that said Clara had a screw loose. "How'd you meet someone in the yard?"

"Shh!"

"Sorry." Tammy clapped her hand over her mouth. Then she whispered, "What happened?"

"This spot is great, Tam. You gotta come with me next time. I'll go back tomorrow, since…Uncle Harris will be here."

Tammy nodded grimly. She knew the drill. Sometimes, weekends weren't easy. Other days, Uncle Harris was in a good mood. But since they could never tell when he'd be happy or angry, they just steered clear as often as possible. Safer that way.

"So, there's this awesome little clearing. And the moss was so soft there, and it wasn't buggy, so I laid down and took a nap. And then I woke up and there was a guy looking down at me."

"What!" Tammy hissed, her eyes turning round and filling with amazement.

"I almost lost it, but then I stopped because I didn't want Uncle Harris to hear me. Anyway, we got to talking. His name is Gaven. He seems real nice."

Tammy's eyes narrowed. It was clear she was catching on. "*That's* why you're really going back tomorrow, isn't it? You want to see him again. What was he doing out there?"

Clara's cheeks heated. "I…I'm not really sure why he was there. But Tammy, I never talk to anyone other than you. And neither do you! We never get out of here. Don't you want to come with me and meet him?"

She shook her head, her movements rapid, showing her avid discontent. "If Daddy found out, I'd get in trouble. And so would you. I don't think you should go out there again. How far away were you?"

"Just at the edge of the property, way back behind the house. The wall is broken back there, Tammy. We could—"

"We could what? Sneak out?" At first, the idea seemed to excite her. Then her lip trembled as she tugged Clara close. "No, no, I can't. Daddy would beat my butt. He'd *hurt* me. He'd hurt you, too. You know it. Please don't go, Clara. Please stay with me."

When tears leaked from her eyes and down her soft, rosy cheeks, Clara held her tight and soothed her. Sometimes Tammy acted so much older than she was, and other times, she seemed younger. Her fear was palpable; she rarely left her room, and when she did, it was only to eat dinner or get another book from upstairs.

Books were her companions, Clara knew. The same rang true for her. Neither of the girls knew anyone. They were homeschooled, shielded from the rest of the world.

But Clara had met someone.

She didn't know if she could trust him, she didn't know if he was even real or if she'd made him up.

But she knew one thing—he was someone else to talk to.

And she wouldn't give that up. She'd go see him again tomorrow. Even if it meant risking her uncle's wrath. Tammy didn't have to know about it; maybe it was best to keep it from her in the future. The girl was fragile, broken.

Then again, so was Clara.

She wanted to heal, to get out. And maybe Gaven could help pave the way.

Chapter Ten

"Well. Bye." Gaven turned to leave, his gait as wooden and robotic as ever, when Daniel placed a firm hand on his shoulder.

"Wait a second, where are you headed off to so quick? Breakfast ain't done yet." Daniel nodded in the direction of the tiny kitchen, where pancakes sizzled on the griddle. The heady scent of bacon wafted up from the pan.

"I'm going for a walk. In the woods."

"In the woods?" Tiny lines reached out over Daniel's cheeks when his lips rose in warm amusement. "Thought you were a city boy. What'd you like about the woods so much yesterday?"

"Like I told you. I just enjoyed the walk."

"Well, before you enjoy another walk. Sit down and have some pancakes and bacon. I know your mom ain't never cooked like this."

"No, she didn't." Gaven obligingly dragged a chair away from the little dining table off the kitchen, and sat down. "Mom's more of a Pop Tarts and Cheerios kind of woman."

Daniel shook his head as he plopped down across from Gaven, placing plates piled with steaming, delicious-smelling food in front of them. "Your mother never was too good of a cook. But don't tell her I said that."

"I won't." Gaven forced a quick smirk.

Facial expressions, like emotions, were difficult for him, but he managed to create a façade that worked most of the time. He knew he couldn't do it naturally like other people, but at least he made an attempt. He likened himself the man in Albert Camus's *The Stranger*, all at once odd and unable to fit according to society's standards.

Most people didn't like that kind of person. So why had Clara Pendleton seemed to enjoy his company? He had to figure her out; it bugged him he hadn't been able to compartmentalize her personality to the categories he'd found useful for others of the human species. It didn't bug him on an emotional level, but a quizzical, scientific level. He had to see her. He had to know.

Discomfort crawled through him, making him realize there might be another motive for his desire to talk with her.

Loneliness.

She sparked something within him he'd never before experienced, and that made him almost queasy.

"Gaven. Staring at your breakfast won't work. You have to actually chew it. Just saying."

"Oh." He straightened in his chair, his eyes hooded from the medication. He hated the pills; he swore they only made him crazier. He dug into his breakfast obediently, then with more vigor when he realized how scrumptious it was. His uncle really could cook. Living with this guy certainly meant he'd never go hungry.

After drenching the pancakes in syrup, he savored each fluffy bite until the plate was clean. Daniel was only halfway through his own breakfast, and he seemed to marvel at how quickly Gaven had eaten.

"You'll give yourself a stomachache, inhaling it like that," Daniel warned.

"That's okay. I have to go." Gaven stood abruptly, watching his uncle's expression for any sign of suspicion. His mother would've been suspicious; she'd never trusted him.

Daniel just looked at him with that same benevolent, easygoing acknowledgement and acquiesced with a simple shrug of one shoulder. "Have a great day, Gav." Then he picked up the dishes and took them into the kitchen to wash them.

Have a great day? Gaven hurried down the steps and into the parking lot. *Nobody ever means it when they say that. But the preposterous thing is, I think Uncle Dan actually* does *mean it. Shit, imagine that.*

Gaven rushed instinctively along the same path he'd taken before, and located the trail he'd followed without much difficulty. It was a beautiful day, with few clouds in the sky, perhaps seventy-five degrees. Since his arrival, he'd heard locals complaining about the heat—which was nothing compared to a South Florida summer.

He was chilly, so he'd brought a jacket with him. As he warmed up, he slipped it off and tied it around his narrow waist. Clad in a white t-shirt and khaki cargo pants, he traversed the narrow trail with ease and soon found himself at the half-broken wall.

Disappointment lodged itself within his chest.

She wasn't there.

Chapter Eleven

She emerged from the shrubs and clambered to her feet, clad in an older pair of jeans she hoped Aunt Nan wouldn't notice as much. She knew she'd be getting dirty climbing through the bushes, so she'd purposefully worn old clothes, including a plain blue t-shirt she'd dug out of the bottom of her dresser drawer.

As she straightened and looked out over the wall, she saw a figure moving steadily away. "Gaven!" Not loud enough. "Gaven!" This time, he turned.

The look on his face was one of surprise—not elation, not happiness. There was something different about him she couldn't quite figure out. He stalked toward her purposefully.

"You're here," he said.

"Well, yes. I said I would be."

"I'm from the school of thought that a person doesn't usually mean it when they make a promise."

"Is that your experience?" she countered.

"Yes."

"Well, you'd better get used to *truth* with me. I'm brutally honest. And when I tell you I'll meet you somewhere, I mean it." She smiled, reaching out to take his hand. A bold move on her part, but something about him made her want to be close to him. His hand was soft, his palm a tad clammy. For some reason, she felt as if she'd been here before. As if it had already happened. "I'm not sure why, but I like you a lot."

"I like you a lot, too." He sat on the wall, still holding her hand, and she leaned against the stonework. "Why don't we go for a walk?"

He released her and stood straight and tall, his movements reminding her of an android in a science fiction novel. She cocked her head, observing him, while his deep brown eyes bore through her as if absorbing her very essence.

"I…I can't," she mumbled.

"Why not?"

"I have to stay here."

"Okay." He sat on the wall again. "Why?"

"I don't…I d-d-d-don't really g-g-go anywhere." She sat down beside him. The wall was wide enough they could lean back to back, and so they did, each staring off into separate worlds like sentinels surveying their respective domains.

"You're stuttering, like yesterday," he stated, his tone flat.

"Yes."

"Why? Have you had this problem for a long time?"

She nodded. "Whenever I…whenever I talk about things…I mean, if I…"

"If you're uncomfortable, you stutter," he finished. "Can I ask you something?"

"Yes." She turned slightly so she could look at him.

"Why are you here in Clearwater?"

"I've lived here since I was six."

"You said that, but you didn't say why." He peered into her eyes.

She shrugged. "It's nice to talk to someone. You can ask me anything. But...I...no one has asked me about...anything before."

"When you said you don't get out, you mean...you *really* don't get out at all ever, do you?"

"How'd you know?"

"Simple. You talk to me like I'm a normal person, you look at me..." He smirked. "I like the way you look at me."

"So? I don't understand." Clara frowned. Sure, there was something unusual about him, but she found his mannerisms appealing. His energy comforted her somehow; at first, she'd thought it was because she was content to finally be around another person, but she quickly realized it was *him* she liked, not just the fact she was no longer alone.

"Most people treat me differently," he explained. "Because I have Asperger's."

"What...what is that? I'm sorry...I don't know." Clara felt her face flush in embarrassment. The word itself—*Asperger's*—seemed so foreign to her, and she wasn't sure if what he was revealing was private or not. Was he showing her a part of himself he normally hid? And why? Why had he chosen *her* of all people?

"It's a form of autism. I have difficulty expressing emotion. And things like this, what we're doing now—interacting isn't easy for me."

"My Uncle Harris watches Star Trek."

"Data." Gaven had a faraway look on his face, but he clearly recalled the character.

"I was going to say Spock." Clara giggled. "But I don't understand why it's a bad thing. I like you the way you are." She took his hand again, squeezing it gently.

"You're the first who does."

Something in that moment resonated with her. Later, she would realize she'd fallen in love with him that very day. But like Gaven himself, she couldn't express it.

And she didn't even try.

Chapter Twelve

"Come with me," he urged, but his voice was level, failing to reveal any hint of passion or desperation. He wished he could express himself better, but the damn medication made it so much harder. "We don't have to hang out by this wall all day."

They'd been talking for almost an hour, but she mostly asked him questions, and he spent a lot of time suspecting her motives.

He could've walked away, but he was too curious. Or maybe it was something more.

Something inside him begged to know more about her, to figure her out. He wanted to analyze her personality, put her beneath his microscope, and discover what she was all about.

It bothered him that he couldn't pinpoint her. Most people gave themselves away quickly; he could tell what kind of a person they were in moments. He'd long since decided this was because they were shallow, but perhaps it was something else.

Maybe they were just open to it. Open emotionally, the way he wasn't. Sometimes, he envied them. What was it like to be normal, to be the way his mother wanted him to be?

He started to turn and walk away, but Clara didn't move. She wasn't going to be dragged anywhere.

"Come on."

"I c-c-c-can't." Her eyes began to water, and she still stood on the inside of the ivy-covered wall, her hand in his, reaching out as if she wanted to go. But her feet were planted firmly on that moss, and the hesitancy—the *fear*—in her eyes ran deep. Deeper than anything he'd ever seen before.

There. There it lay. The *truth* in Clara's soul.

He stepped close to her again. "I see you."

"What?"

"I'm almost there. I almost have you figured out. Will you come with me?" He knew he should try something romantic—*isn't that what people do?*—but he didn't have it in him. If only he could sort out what he had in his head, maybe he could understand why he was drawn to her and what to do about it. But all he could do was stand there, feeling childish, tugging on her hand in the hopes she might follow.

"What if—"

"What if you get caught?" he interrupted. "Then what? You said you live with your aunt and uncle. Don't you go out anywhere?"

"No."

"Don't you have friends?"

"No."

"I don't have any friends, but you should have friends. Why don't you?"

"*You* don't have friends?"

He shook his head. "That is extraneous."

"Why doesn't a handsome, intelligent, sweet guy like you have friends?"

He might've blushed. He averted his eyes, feeling the corner of his mouth rise in a slight smile.

Clara giggled. "You don't realize how handsome you are, do you? When you smile, this dimple appears in your cheek." With her other hand, she reached up and gently brushed her finger along his skin, making him shiver. "I can see you're uncomfortable around me, but—"

"No," he said firmly, wanting to clarify. "I *am* comfortable around you. That's what's strange to me. That's what I'm having trouble figuring out. I like the way I feel around you."

"This is only the second time you've met me."

"I like…I like being around you," he hazarded. "I…I have trouble explaining. But…there's something about you. You seem to…understand me. You've had very little contact with the outside world. Maybe that's in my favor. Maybe you're unspoiled by society, or because of being sheltered your perceptions of *normal* and *abnormal* are different than most people's."

"What if I were just using you as a way to get out?"

She was testing the waters; he could tell. He shook his head, knowing from the look in her eye that such a thing would be impossible. "You genuinely like me. I can see it."

"You're right. I do." A rosy hue spread across her cheeks and nose. She averted her eyes in her nervousness.

"Come with me," he said again.

"Out there?"

"Yes, out there. In Clearwater. It's a tiny little town, the people are nice. Trust me. I just got here, but it's not that bad."

She turned and looked over her shoulder, toward the estate.

"What's holding you back?" he asked.

"Uncle Harris." When her gaze met his, he knew something bad had happened. Whatever it was, he couldn't figure out. He hoped she would tell him. But first, he had to get her out of the woods.

"Come into town with me. There's this little coffee place—Express Ohh, I think it's called. I'll get you a drink." He watched her turn again and look at the house. "If you're worried about being home at a certain time, I'm wearing a watch."

"It's not that. I just don't want anyone to see me and tell him where I am. I'm not supposed to be out."

"What could he do?"

"Everything." Terror flashed through her ocean blue eyes. "He's a councilman for Jackson Hole…and he's a retired state representative with connections."

"So?"

"So, no one can touch him. *No one.*"

Chapter Thirteen

Clara trembled as she climbed precariously over the crumbling stone wall.

Gaven held her hand, helping her over, and as she made the last step, she stumbled, falling forward against his chest. His warmth was unmistakable, the energy that flowed between them purely magnetic; she couldn't resist him and she wasn't sure why.

He was older than her, and Tammy would've been horrified to see the way Clara pressed her small hands against his narrow chest, staring into his chocolate brown eyes. She saw things in his eyes she'd never seen before— a world she couldn't remember, pain that was just as horrific as her own.

He was a kindred spirit.

She knew immediately he was her soul mate.

For a long moment, she stared into his eyes, and he stared back. She was so close she could've kissed his tantalizing, full lips. Instead, she just froze.

"You don't have to worry about me," he finally said. "I won't take advantage of you."

"Why?" Catching herself, she stammered, "I m-m-mean, w-w-what do you mean?"

"I'm not like other men. I'm all cerebral. Sex means nothing to me."

She didn't know why she'd said it, but the words tumbled from her lips, "I'm a virgin." Shocked at her admission to this near-stranger, she clapped a hand over her mouth.

"Of course you are," he said, seemingly unaffected. "You've never left this place before. But—" He remained silent for a long moment. Then he took her hand and began leading her along the narrow path through the woods. "Something happened to you, I can see it. You've never had sexual intercourse, but something *has* happened to you, and you don't want to talk about it. You hide it."

"Why do you say it like that?"

"What do you mean?"

"I mean, in the movies and in books, people just say *sex*. You talk about it like…like a textbook."

He chuckled. "I told you, I'm cerebral. My intellect is more important to me. You know that already. You can feel it."

"Yes, that's true. I like it."

He forged ahead, holding her behind him until he cleared a branch out of the way. The sun shone down, dancing over bright green foliage, brightening the forest floor.

"I don't know why we've met, but I'm glad we did. You came right to me," Clara said. "I opened my eyes and there you were. How interesting. Like in a book."

"You read a lot, like me."

"Yes, I love to read. One thing I'll say for Uncle Harris, he's always kept books in the house. The place has been in the family for several generations, and every generation added books to the library upstairs. My cousin, Tammy, and I read a lot."

"There's so much more to your story, Clara. I'm waiting to hear it."

The rest of the path was clear, and they walked hand in hand for a while until Gaven complained his hands were sweaty. He seemed uncomfortable with physical contact, but at the same time, he seemed to want her near him; a fascinating juxtaposition that did not escape her.

The most mind-boggling thing was that she barely knew this man, yet he'd coaxed her away from her uncle's property. After only two lengthy conversations, two afternoons of discovering they were twin souls, Gaven had managed to talk her into climbing over the wall and out of her prison.

She wondered if he knew how huge this was.

If he didn't realize it, he would soon.

As they crossed the grassy field outside the forest, he pointed out Winterbloom Bed and Breakfast. "I met Chloe Sheppard the other day. Interesting woman."

"And you figured her out?" Clara liked the change of topic; if he distracted her with other discussions, getting her away from her uncle's property became a bit easier. She wondered if he realized that, as well.

"Yes. I can map out anyone's personality traits and character in my mind in—" He tapped his temple. "Usually under thirty minutes." He stopped for a moment, eyeing her, before shoving his hands in his pockets and continuing.

Out of fear, she stuck close to him, hyper-aware of her surroundings and the reality that she'd *never* been out alone. Not once.

"You aren't so simple," he continued. "You perplex me."

"Is that why you dragged me out here? I mean, because I perplex you? I hope I'm not an experiment of yours, Gaven. That would make me sad."

"No. You're not an experiment."

"Then you genuinely wanted to be near me today?"

"Yes."

A part of her was terrified. She wanted to turn and run, but she didn't know where to run to. Desperate to grab onto the only thing nearby she could even begin to comprehend, she wrapped her hand around Gaven's and let him lead her toward Downtown Clearwater.

A million thoughts threatened to overtake her. She was sure her heart would slam through her ribcage if she let it.

She'd climbed over that rock wall and left her uncle's estate.

What if he found out somehow?

The dread tore through her stomach, tying her in knots. Every hair on the back of her neck stood on end as they walked past a café and a daycare, where a few women caught her eye. She looked away quickly.

This was a small town, not like where she was born. Word would spread fast. They would wonder who she was and—

"Oh, G-G-G-Gaven, I d-d-d-don't like thi…this." She gasped, barely able to get the words out. They walked slowly, but she felt as if she were moving too fast.

Burning up.

Her flesh was on fire. All she could see was Uncle Harris coming toward her in the dark. So many times she'd offered herself up, sacrificed herself to protect Tammy. He would own her again. What could she do about it?

Nothing.

Because he was *King* in that world, and she was meaningless. He'd told her that a thousand times, the words now emblazoned on her mind, tattooed forever into her subconscious.

Before she could react, turn, and run, Gaven pulled her into a little storefront and she found herself standing in a café decorated in mocha and tan colors, with little booths and a bar area. A woman behind the front counter of the small establishment glanced at them, her brow furrowed in concern, before Gaven whisked Clara toward a corner booth and sat beside her.

"Do you realize you're breathing heavily?" Gaven asked.

She noticed it; he was right. Her chest was heaving and she was gasping. "I…w-w-w-what's wrong with me." She tried to keep her voice down.

He squeezed her thigh. "You're having a panic attack. Take a deep breath."

She did as he suggested, then let the breath out raggedly.

"Count to ten, slowly," Gaven instructed, his hand on her back.

"One…two…three…four…" She continued until she reached ten. The heady aroma of coffee filled her nostrils, and it calmed her.

After a little while, she was okay. And that was when a slim woman with long brown hair and bright green eyes bounced over to their table. She wore a mocha apron to match the décor and seemed as if she were running on caffeine.

"Hello, I'm Jennifer, owner of Express Ohh's. Can I get you two anything?"

"Two iced lattes," Gaven said, his hand still on Clara's back.

Clara didn't look up.

"Is she okay?" Jennifer asked.

"She will be. She just doesn't feel good."

"Okay, well, let me get your drinks. And you two let me know if you need anything else."

Clara averted her gaze; she didn't want to talk to anyone but Gaven. She wasn't ready for that yet, and she was too afraid of her uncle's influence. What if he drove through here? What if he saw her? She had no idea where he went during the day, or if he was still at the house.

When she glanced up, she inadvertently met Jennifer's wary gaze, then glanced away.

The last thing she needed was a stranger's suspicion.

Chapter Fourteen

Jennifer stepped into the back room, watching from a distance.

There was something unusual about the young couple who'd just rushed, harried, into her shop. The young man moved woodenly and had an oddness about him she couldn't quite define. He'd urged the girl inside and brought her to a booth, where she stammered and began having a panic attack.

Something was wrong.

She didn't want to jump the gun, but she had a feeling. An unsettling sensation sank over her. She knew just about everyone in town, but not this girl. She'd seen the man at least once, and thought he might be a recent arrival in Clearwater.

As soon as she heard the voice on the other end, she said, "Are you anywhere nearby?"

"Jennifer." Sheriff Ryan Ryder's deep voice cut through her concerns, making her exhale in relief. "There's been a little fender-bender. I'm handling it with Deputy Sheppard."

"Does that mean you can stop by the shop?"

"Why, what's wrong?"

"Nothing...exactly."

"Come on, Jennifer, you know I don't like people beatin' around the bush. Tell me what's going on."

"Not much." She snuck from the room into the little office in the back of the shop and closed the door. "Real quick, I'm just concerned about this young couple that came into Express Ohh's a minute ago. The girl was having a panic attack, and the guy seemed…weird."

"Weird how? Was he bothering her?"

"I don't think so. I…I have to get back out front. But can you please come by?"

"Sure, I'll be there as soon as I can."

"Thanks, Ryan."

The line went dead. Jennifer stared at the screen of her phone for a moment before she headed back out front.

The couple was gone.

"Why did we just leave?" Gaven wondered as they stepped around the side of the building.

"You d-d-don't understand," Clara retorted firmly. "I think you should know m-m-m-more about me before y-y-you…before anything."

Every word sounded like a chore for her. He was beginning to *see* Clara, figure her out. But she was different. And special. He wondered if she knew.

"Tell me." They leaned against the brick façade of Express Ohh's, just around the corner in a narrow, well-kept alley, so no one would see them.

She took a deep breath, and spoke slowly. "Uncle Harris lost it when my parents were killed. Tammy, my cousin, was drawn into the whole thing, only because she's never been allowed to go to public school because of everything that happened. My uncle decided it was unsafe, so Aunt Nan homeschooled us."

"Unsafe…What happened?"

The pain in Clara's eyes rang clear as day. If Gaven had been able to *feel*, truly sense every emotion she had, he'd have felt that pain and it would've pierced him deeply. Because of the medication he was on, he could barely scratch the surface, and he fought for that one emotion that would connect him to her; he fought so hard for it. It barely came. He clenched his fists in the pockets of his khakis, frustrated with himself and the medication.

She forged on.

"Mom and Dad were both teachers at the same elementary school. I went to a different school. Anyway…they…t-t-they were at school w-w-when…they were…k-k-k-killed."

In her broken words, she described it as best she could, her eyes brimming with tears that refused to fall.

He imagined it, pictured every moment.

The gunman entering the school, brandishing the weapon, having lost his mind.

Why? Because of the meds. Because he wanted to die. The drugs increased his craze, drove him closer to the edge. He'd already lost it, but the pills nudged him to the precipice.

He'd held the kids at gunpoint, threatened the principal. Somebody tried to run.

Bang, bang.

One kid down. *Shit*, he was only a second-grader.

Braden Pendleton, Clara's father, stepped carefully into the path of the weapon while the child drowned in his own blood.

"You don't want to do this, son," Braden had said.

Later on, the school nurse had told Clara how brave her father was, repeating word for word his calm coaxing, every syllable he'd used in an attempt to save the children—and the gunman, because the killer himself was only a child. Seventeen.

It didn't do any good.

The gunman shot and killed Braden, and when his wife, Lynette, sobbed and ran to his broken, bleeding body, the gunman killed her, too.

All while Clara had been at school across town.

She told Gaven she remembered hating herself for having a good day, not knowing her parents were dead.

He wanted to make her feel better, but he didn't know how. She leaned against him, then dragged his arms around her until he was holding her. Together, they leaned against the brick wall.

"Where did this happen?" Gaven asked.

"Near Okeechobee, Florida," she whispered.

"What?"

"Okee—"

"No, I heard you." When she looked up at him, her gaze questioning, he added, "*I'm* from Florida, too."

"Where?"

"West Palm Beach."

"How'd you get here?"

"It's a long story." He kept his arms around her because he could tell she needed it. Even though it made him uncomfortable.

"Tell me. I have time."

"Why are you holding onto me like this?" he wondered.

"Don't you know?"

He shook his head.

"It...feels good. No one has ever held me close before...not like this."

"You think I'm normal because you've never experienced a relationship with a regular person."

She almost laughed, then she seemed to notice he was serious. "You *are* a regular person. There's nothing wrong with you. You're normal."

"Not according to—"

"Forget everyone else," she interrupted, her voice suddenly free of the trembles he'd grown so accustomed to. "You don't care what they think, do you?"

"No."

"Gaven, I don't see a man who has a disability, or a disorder, or whatever it is they call Asperger's. I see a brilliant, handsome..." She blushed, lowering her gaze. "I like you a lot. You're sweet. I knew it right away...well, after you scared me a bit."

"Sorry about that."

"It doesn't matter anymore. I like being around you. I've never been so comfortable around anyone before, except Tammy. It's like...like you understand me."

Her gaze met his, and his stomach churned for a reason he couldn't identify. It bothered him he couldn't put these things into phrases; it was as if he was always standing on the edge of some great discovery, but it was just out of his reach. He knew what had taken it away—the drugs. They controlled him. But something about Clara's presence seemed to set him free.

"Finally," he muttered.

"What?"

"Finally, someone who gets me!"

"That's what I was saying." She smirked. "Why do these things happen, do you think? I mean, random meetings like this. How strange of you to wander into the woods and find me."

"I'm not sure. The Universe conspired to bring us together." He paused, then added, "You don't talk like a seventeen-year-old girl."

She shrugged. "I guess to talk like a seventeen-year-old, I'd have to spend more time around them to know how they talk."

"True." He snuggled his head against her shoulder, and she ran her fingers through his hair. Beyond the alley, in front of the coffee shop, he heard a heavy door slam—like a truck—but he ignored it. "I started going out a lot even before I turned twenty-one, hanging out at bars, drinking, trying to mingle. I thought if I put myself out in *normal* crowds, it would make me normal somehow. It didn't."

"I told you, you *are* normal, Gaven. Normal in a way I think is wonderful."

"If you get along with me, you're not normal, either."

She eyed him playfully, scrunching up her nose. "Keep talking."

Tucking his head back against hers, he continued. "I was threatened at a bar one day. But the mood stabilizers I'm on don't allow me to get angry. I don't feel much of anything, like I told you before. I'm a mess, Clara."

"Let me be the judge of that."

Somewhere within him, he felt pleasure as she ran her hands up and down his back, giving him a gentle massage. "I got into a fight. I had to protect myself. Logic won out, but I didn't. My mother sent me here to live with her brother, Uncle Daniel. She said she couldn't handle me anymore. I know she just wanted to get rid of me."

Her body tensed against his. "What about your dad?"

"I don't know him. Mom never married, and my father—whoever he was—didn't stick around."

"I'm sorry."

"Don't be. I'd rather not have him in my life, anyway."

He withdrew, letting her slip her hand into his, and started to walk toward the mouth of the alley. He stopped when he heard voices, pressing his arm against Clara to hold her steady.

Lifting his finger to his mouth, Gaven shot a piercing gaze in her direction.

"I'll keep an eye out for them, Jennifer," a heavy male voice was saying. "I just want to make sure these kids are okay. But the way you describe this guy, he sounds like Daniel Bridge's nephew."

"Are you sure?" Gaven recognized Jennifer's voice, the woman who owned Express Ohh's.

"Yeah, probably. I'm not going to worry about it now, though."

"Shouldn't you talk to Daniel?"

"Nah, there's nothing to say. If it is his nephew, I'm sure he's fine."

"And the girl?"

There was a pause.

"I don't know about her. Guess we'll have to wait and see."

Gaven and Clara stayed still for a long minute or two while a truck door shut and an engine roared to life. The two emerged from the alley to find the vehicle had gone.

Clara seemed terrified.

"Are you all right?" Gaven asked.

"If my uncle finds out I left—"

"You said he's a politician in the next town or something?"

"Yes."

"Why are you so afraid of him?"

"Come on. Let's walk and talk. I'll tell you. Oh, God. I'll tell you everything…"

Chapter Fifteen

Her heart pounded, but she didn't cry. She couldn't fathom why she was telling these things to a man she'd only just met. But it was like he'd said—the Universe had decided it, not her.

And so she told him what Uncle Harris had done.

How he'd relapsed into alcoholism, how he'd *touched* her. How Tammy's growth had been stunted because of his abuse, and how Aunt Nan had turned her head as if nothing was going on.

She ran her hand along the self-help books in Happy Ever After, Clearwater's bookstore. She'd never been here before; the scent of freshly printed pages filled her nostrils. It didn't smell musty or old like the books in her uncle's library.

"These things can't help me," she mumbled, her voice soft.

Gaven's shoulder brushed against hers. "What?"

"I'm trapped." She kept her voice low, for fear someone would hear her. "I'm...I'm not even supposed to...t-t-to be here." Her eyes widened. "What—"

"We've been gone two hours," he said, seemingly anticipating her question. "Don't worry so much."

"Gaven, you don't understand. He could...he could hurt me."

"I have an idea." Gaven's calculating expression gave way to a scheme.

"What's that?"

"Come home with me."

"B-b-but you l-l-live with your uncle."

"He'll understand, I think. He's not like my mother. It's time for you to get help, Clara."

"This is all happening too fast."

He slipped his hand around hers, tugging her toward the exit. "That's because the Universe conspired to bring us together, remember? Now, it's going to help *you*."

It was a waking nightmare.

The vivid memory tore at her insides, making her want to vomit.

Escape wasn't all it was cracked up to be. There was something to be said for being locked away in her dark room.

But it wasn't safe. It never had been.

She'd lost count of how many nights she'd been unable to sleep, laying there under the covers against a mattress that was soft and inviting. She was too frightened to close her eyes. Sometimes she tried to pretend the comforter was an impenetrable barrier, and she wrapped it around her body, getting herself so tied up in it she was sure she wouldn't be able to get out in the morning.

But he still broke through.

That's when she'd learned to jump out of her body, to be somewhere else, *someone* else.

The few memories she had of her parents would resurface, and she'd hold onto them as though they were a life raft helping her tread water.

She'd blurted out to Gaven that she was a virgin. That was true. Had she been touched? Oh yes, she had.

The stench of Uncle Harris's liquor breath hovered over her as he told her *be quiet* and *I'm doing this for your own good.* Confusing it with affection, she'd learned to accept it when it began after her eleventh birthday, but the horrors only worsened, the nightmares following her every waking moment.

Now she covered her ears and closed her eyes tightly, a ritual she'd picked up to calm herself. Drifting further and further into her own mind, where she found distorted peace, Clara disconnected herself from the world around her.

Until something brought her back.

Someone's hand on her shoulder.

Gaven.

Chapter Sixteen

She snapped her eyes open, taking in the brick building which housed the town's bar, On the Rocks.

Logic tore through her at incredible speed.

"I can't go in there," she said breathlessly. "I'm seventeen."

Instead of asking her why she'd been covering her ears and looking into her own head, Gaven merely shrugged. Did he get it? Did he understand? If he didn't, he was doing a great job of faking it.

"We're going to talk to Uncle Daniel, that's all. He won't have any problem with you being in the bar, I promise."

He led her inside, where dim lighting made it seem later in the day than it really was. The bar was decorated with antique signs and advertisements, and a framed print of Norman Rockwell's *The Runaway* hung on the wall behind the cash register.

Gaven nudged Clara and said, "Uncle Dan loves Rockwell. I dislike it."

"Why?"

"Not sure." He frowned as he approached the bar, dismissing small-talk.

A young woman popped up from behind the counter, a washcloth in her hand. Her short, mussed-up brown hair framed a lovely round face with bright emerald eyes. She grinned wide.

"Hey, folks!" She leaned over the counter. "Hi, Gaven."

"Hello, Lisa. I want you to meet my friend, Clara. Clara, this is Lisa."

"Nice to meet you, Clara. What can I get for you?"

Without any preamble, a man's voice called out from the other side of the room. "Lisa, you're too young to be a bartender." The handsome older man walked up to the bar, combing his auburn hair with his fingers. Then he thrust his hand toward Clara. "Hello, and you are...?"

"Clara." She shook his hand after a brief hesitation, telling herself to act as normal as possible. But all she could think about was Uncle Harris.

"I'm Daniel Bridge, but you can call me Dan. I own this bar, and—" He clapped a hand on Gaven's shoulder. "I'm this brilliant young man's proud uncle." When Gaven gave him a suspicious glance, Daniel added, "It's true, kid. Better get used to it."

Lisa scrunched up her button nose and grumbled. "Why can't I bartend?"

"Because you're seventeen, that's why, and everyone in this town knows it."

"I'm just trying to make a little extra money, that's all." Lisa stuck out her tongue at Daniel. "Mom says there's no room for me at Kate's Salon where she works."

"Well, not to embarrass you in front of visitors, but...you did lose your last cleaning job, *sooo*..."

Clara watched as Lisa huffed and began washing some glasses.

"You clean?" Clara asked. "I mean, for work?"

"Yeah. I couldn't quite cut it in school, so I got my G.E.D. instead. I'm trying to save money to get my own place. But Dan's right, I did lose my last job in…well, an unusual way." The glasses clinked together in the soapy water while she worked.

Clara slumped against the bar, sitting on a stool, and Gaven sat beside her.

"You kids want a drink? Non-alcoholic, of course." Daniel winked at Clara, then gestured to the empty bar. "We're usually slow this time of day."

"I don't…I d-d-don't have any money," Clara mumbled.

"That's okay," Daniel said, eyeing her with increasing interest. "It's on me." He quickly poured the drinks and slid them across the counter.

Gaven sipped at his soda while Clara eyed the girl who was still busy scrubbing things behind the counter.

"How'd you lose your cleaning job?" Clara asked. "I mean, if you don't mind talking about it."

"Oh, no biggie." Lisa shrugged, then giggled.

"Kary's got her hands full with this one," Daniel said, nudging Lisa. By way of explanation, he added, "You're new in town, I see. Kary is Lisa's mother, and she works at the salon with her sister, Kate. Kate's the owner."

"Ah, I see." Clara leaned over the counter, feeling a bit more comfortable. "So, what happened?"

"Well." Lisa began drying glasses. "I had this great cleaning job at a place just at the edge of town. Real rich people. It didn't last long. I had to clean the bathroom, and I have my own bathroom at Mom's house…well, I cleaned the shower just like I clean mine and—"

"Naked?" Clara interrupted.

"How'd you know?" Lisa's brow furrowed.

Excitement rose in Clara's belly as she realized who this young woman was. "Oh my God, did you clean for the Pendletons?"

"Yeah…"

"I'm Clara Pendleton!" Her stomach flipped. "I mean…I l-l-live there." She flushed, suddenly realizing she'd said too much. If Uncle Harris found out—

"You're visiting?" Lisa asked, her eyes wide.

"No, I'm their niece."

"And you just arrived in town?" Daniel asked.

"No." Clara glanced over at Gaven, whose face was expressionless. "I've lived here since I was six with my cousin."

Lisa and Daniel exchanged a curious glance.

"Oh." Daniel frowned. "How come I've never seen you in town?"

"I…I d-d-don't leave home much." Realizing she was starting to stutter again, she began to answer their questions with brief nods or gestures.

Soon, they stopped asking.

But they looked worried, suspicious.

Reaching over beneath the bar, so no one could see them, she took Gaven's hand. She needed his touch; he comforted her. Even though they'd just met, the connection was strong.

It thrilled her. And terrified her.

As quick as she could, she urged him out of that place, suddenly afraid of these people who seemed so well-meaning.

She had to get home before Uncle Harris knew she was missing.

Chapter Seventeen

"You could've talked to him, Clara. Why didn't you?"

Gaven's stare was unrelenting, as if he bore straight into her soul. They hurried down the road toward Winterbloom Bed and Breakfast and the long driveway that wound through the woods and into the Pendleton estate. The path they'd taken from the broken section of rock wall wrapped around the property and toward the road; Clara hadn't realized it until now.

She took long strides through the field and toward the little path they'd followed.

"Clara, I asked you a question."

She returned his stare, drawn in by his deep gaze. "I c-c-c-can't."

"This is your chance to escape." They walked slower as they forged through the forest. "You can get out of this." He spoke evenly, every word edged with logic.

She stopped for a moment, clapping her hands over her ears and squeezing her eyes shut.

Sometimes, the darkness overwhelmed her.

She couldn't take it.

Opening her eyes again, she realized Gaven was standing in front of her, analyzing her as though he were searching for something.

"You're broken." Gaven's observation sliced through her, and she gasped. Before she could say anything, he added, "This can be fixed."

His movements were slow, calculated. As if he'd watched a movie, or read a book, that taught him how to move forward, how to take her hands in his.

How to kiss her.

She'd never been kissed before, so she had nothing to compare it to. He pressed his lips against hers for a long moment, but his eyes were open as if to observe her reaction.

Her breath hitched and she enjoyed the momentary warmth before he pulled away, letting go of her hands.

"How do you know?" she whispered.

He turned and headed down the path, leading the way. "I just do."

The ivy wall seemed almost threatening. It marked the separation between this world and the next, the barrier that stood between freedom and imprisonment.

On this side, she was safe—but alone.

On that side, she had a place to live, a roof over her head. But she had to protect Tammy, and shielding her cousin meant sacrificing her body to a drunk whose memory the next day would be hazy, at best.

She flashed back to Uncle Harris, and how he'd stand at the kitchen table in the morning, holding his coffee cup, usually saying the same thing each time as if nothing had happened: "Good morning, Clara. You're looking nice today."

Nice. Defiled was more like it. Destroyed. She had nothing left to give.

And here she was, about to climb over that disintegrating wall and return to the horrors she'd been putting up with since she was eleven years old.

She wanted to knock down that wall, crush every rock in her way. Could she? Could she even dare?

"Clara. Come back. Your mind is drifting."

She turned and looked at Gaven, who stood beside her with his hands in the pockets of his khakis.

"I'm sorry. I was thinking."

"You're scared."

"Yes. I'm afraid of him."

Gaven didn't question her. He knew enough of what was going on, and he seemed determined to help her. How he could, she didn't know. As far as she was concerned, she was doomed.

She wrapped her arms around him, and he was slow to return her embrace.

"I have difficulty with affection," he admitted.

"I know. It's okay."

To her, Gaven was normal—just a regular guy. But then, she'd never known any other man. Somehow, she knew that even if she met someone else, she'd still want to be with Gaven.

"When can I see you again?" he asked.

"Tomorrow?"

"Sure."

She clambered over the wall slowly, aware that every move was reluctant. She didn't want to leave him. Standing on the other side of the wall, she reached out and squeezed his hand. "I'll see you soon. Right here."

"Right here," he repeated, the corner of his mouth turning up, revealing the endearing dimple in his cheek.

"See you then."

And with that, she began her slow crawl through the shrubs.

Chapter Eighteen

She didn't realize how late it had gotten.

She snuck through the back entryway at three in the afternoon, creeping into the hall and toward the steps.

"Where've you been?"

She froze, clamming up, her heart in her throat. Turning, she found Aunt Nan emerging from one of the first floor bedrooms, a feather duster in her hand.

"Um…outside," Clara mumbled.

"I didn't see you in the yard."

"I f-f-f-found a patch of m-m-moss and…I fell asleep."

Aunt Nan's aging face took on a sympathetic expression, and she patted her niece gently on the shoulder. "While you've been sleeping, I've been cleaning."

"Oh?" Clara breathed a sigh of relief, glad her aunt hadn't questioned her further.

The two women walked through the house and toward the kitchen. "I haven't found another cleaning lady." She waved the feather duster in the air as if emphasizing her annoyance. "After that *girl* got naked in *my* shower…what are you smiling about?"

"Nothing." Clara sucked in her lips, forcing away her amusement. If she let on that she knew Lisa, Aunt Nan would know she'd been in town. "It's just a funny story. That's all."

"Wouldn't be funny if it was you walking in on that full moon."

When Aunt Nan turned to put the feather duster in the closet, Clara snorted.

"What was that?" Her aunt turned, shutting the closet door.

"Nothing. I didn't say anything." She paused, adding, "So, what're you doing now?"

"Getting dinner ready." She shook her head, clucking her tongue as she tied her apron. "You know how your uncle is if he doesn't get dinner on time."

Clara nodded in understanding.

"You'd better make yourself scarce," Aunt Nan advised. "He's not in too good of a mood today."

Clara almost said Uncle Harris was *never* in a good mood, but she kept her mouth shut. Aunt Nan always swore there was a time Uncle Harris was a quiet, reserved man, dedicated to Alcoholics Anonymous and well on the path to improving his life.

But when Clara's parents were murdered, he threw away the Program and slipped back into his drinking habit. He did his job well; supposedly, he was a different person at work. A good councilman. As a state representative, she'd heard he'd been one of the best. But Clara didn't know for sure.

She took her aunt's advice.

After helping out in the kitchen for a few minutes, she hurried to her room, where a pile of books awaited her. She plopped down on her bed and studied psychology, a topic that interested her greatly—perhaps because of her uncle. In her homeschooling studies, Aunt Nan encouraged her to branch out, absorb as much knowledge as she could. She found herself especially interested in abnormal psychology.

She locked her door.

Even though it didn't matter.

If someone wanted to get in, they would. If *he* wanted to get in, he would. She shuddered, her skin crawling.

The scent of Aunt Nan's homemade eggplant parmesan drifted throughout the house. A soft knock came at the door an hour or so later, and her aunt announced supper. In the hallway, Clara shut her bedroom door and turned, nearly colliding with her cousin.

"Where were you all day?" The younger girl appeared intrigued, but—

Clara thought she spotted a hint of jealousy in Tammy's eyes.

"Outside." It might not be a good idea to tell Tammy about her exploits. Maybe it was the way her gaze shimmered, her body language betraying her unrest. Tammy wanted Clara to be happy, but at the same time, Clara wasn't sure if her cousin could handle it.

Happiness.

That was something they weren't familiar with. Though Clara had to admit to herself she'd gotten a taste of it today. Being with Gaven gave her a sensation she'd never experienced before. She had to keep that to herself. In this house, it could be dangerous.

Tammy eyed her with some suspicion, but said nothing. They walked downstairs in silence.

Uncle Harris had changed into a comfortable pair of plaid pajama pants and a black t-shirt. He emerged from the den carrying a half-empty bottle of Bud. He was still sober, she could tell. He hadn't hit the Old Granddad yet. He walked with an even gait and his eyes were bright, laugh lines turning up when he spotted the girls. He ran his hands through Tammy's hair.

"There's my kid. How ya doing?"

"Fine, Dad."

Like always, Tammy's responses were subdued, her gaze far away. She never recoiled at her father's touch, but seemed disarmed by it—as though she wished his affection were always this fatherly, this genuine. He smiled, and Clara noticed the slight stubble on his chin, and the way his receding hairline was beginning to gray.

"You both working hard on your studies?" He eyed Clara with an air of disappointment, as if he expected her to fail.

Goddamn it.

He always looked at her like that, as if she were the runt. She wasn't sure why. Aunt Nan said it was because he worried more about her; he wanted to see her succeed. He wanted Braden Pendleton to be proud of her, from wherever he was—looking down from above, *something* like that.

"Clara, what gives?" Uncle Harris sat down at the head of the table in the spacious dining room adjoining a wide living room. They'd recently knocked down the wall separating the two rooms, and during the day, there was a lot of light in here. Now, it had grown dark. Too dark.

"What?" Clara mumbled, taking her usual seat. She kept her head down, staring at her hands in her lap. As usual, Uncle Harris found this annoying.

"Look at me, kid. I can't stand the way you always come to dinner looking miserable. You've been studying, I hope? I noticed you weren't in your room earlier. Hadn't even cracked your books."

"Harris, dear, please…" Aunt Nan entered the room, placing a heavy dish in the middle of the table, her hands covered in oven mitts. "She took one of her books out back and was studying in the sunlight. You know she likes it outdoors."

"I didn't see her," he retorted.

Clara appreciated her aunt sticking up for her, but she couldn't understand why they had to talk about her as though she weren't there. "I was studying," she said firmly. "I swear I was."

Studying my friendship with Gaven. Trying to figure it out.

Uncle Harris didn't need to know about that. He couldn't. If he ever found out—

Clara shuddered, praying it never came to that.

The conversation changed focus, and Uncle Harris started talking about the book he'd been reading earlier.

"I love these mysteries." He looked up at Aunt Nan, chuckling, a wide smile crossing his once-handsome face. "I like reading them just to see how accurate they are, you know? Some are pretty good."

"What are you reading now, dear?"

He cut through his portion of eggplant parmesan, chewing a piece before saying, "*Death and White Diamonds*, by…uh…" He looked up, trying to think. "Jeff Markowitz, that's the author."

"You like it?"

"Pretty good." He nudged his daughter. "What have you been reading, sunshine?" The pet name was filled with adoration, affection which confused Clara. She couldn't figure him out.

Tammy smiled meekly. *"Twenty Thousand Leagues Under the Sea."*

"Again?" He laughed. "Kid, how many times have you read that book?"

"Three."

"And how many more times are you going to read it? Until you've got it memorized?"

Tammy smirked, and the humor she often concealed emerged. "I was thinking twenty thousand times might do it."

He ruffled her hair, laughing, and for a moment, Clara felt the familiar stab of pain lodging itself in her chest. She missed her dad so much.

As she ate, more out of necessity than appetite, she thought of how ironic it was that Uncle Harris had taken them out of public school, insisted on homeschooling, and sheltered them by not allowing them to leave home or socialize—only to hurt them behind closed doors.

She'd discovered it was wrong only recently.

Sure, it didn't feel right. But she accommodated him because they were family, and family helped each other out. It would've been wrong to reject him. After all, he was her uncle. Her father's brother.

Braden Pendleton's brother.

What would her father say if he knew?

She felt as if she'd betrayed her father, but something told her that was wrong. A voice in her head whispered Uncle Harris was the wrong one, *not* her.

That voice of anger, of determination, had grown stronger today in Clearwater. Clara had never been around so many people. She didn't know she could be attracted to anyone so quickly—anyone at all—and she tried to remember if she'd ever read about soul mates in books. She supposed the term had been tossed around a few times, but she wondered if it was real.

If love was real.

She wondered if a man could really love her, especially since she'd already been broken.

A voice drew her back to the present, and she realized she'd been staring at her dinner, not eating it.

Uncle Harris eyed her with deep concern; she'd seen that face many times before. An expression of kindness, of love, a face her father had probably seen on multiple occasions when the kids were growing up.

Neither boy ever talked about their parents much, of Clara's grandparents. Grandfather Pendleton had supposedly been crass, tight with his money, but a man who cared deeply for the moral values of family, who believed strongly in the union of husband and wife.

What else had he believed in? Clara couldn't help but wonder.

"Clara, are you okay, honey?"

She glanced up at Uncle Harris's gaze. The adoring quality in his eyes was something she missed, but she knew that look would be gone quite soon.

She didn't know how many beers he'd had, but he'd certainly finished the first one she'd seen in his hand.

Uncle Harris was close to becoming the monster.

"I'm okay," she mumbled.

"You sure? You're not eating." Uncle Harris nodded toward her plate. "You know, you're going to be eighteen in a few weeks, honey. You've gotta keep your strength up for all those college applications you'll be filling out." He winked at her, then looked at Aunt Nan. "Homeschooling was always the best thing for these girls. They'll have qualities those other kids won't have. Morals. Values." He took a bite of his dinner, then held his fork tightly in his hand, gesturing each time he spoke. "Kids today don't have values. These girls do. We did a good job, Nancy."

"Yes." Aunt Nan nodded, looking pointedly in Clara's direction. "They'll be just fine."

Chapter Nineteen

A girl's room should be a safe place.

A haven.

Clara's room was a prison. In the dark, she cowered beneath the soft blankets, which should have provided some comfort, but didn't. In her flannel pajamas, she curled up, rubbing her cheek against the scratchiness of the knit blanket her mother had made. Aunt Nan had made sure she'd gotten it after her parents were killed. The blanket was one of the few reminders she had left. One of the few things that spoke of a day long gone, a time when she'd been safe.

Now, she was in the kind of danger no one could protect her from.

She thought of Gaven's insistence that his Uncle Daniel could somehow do something for her. What could he possibly do? Even Aunt Nan wouldn't admit something was going on. Clara had tried to tell her once, but she'd been shot down. There were few times in her life she'd seen Aunt Nan angry, and that had been one of those times. She usually cowered, but on that day, fury had flared up in her eyes.

For some reason, she defended her husband. Maybe she just didn't want to think it was possible.

The light from the moon shone in Clara's bedroom window, casting a pale glow across her bed.

In the hall, wood creaked under heavy footsteps.

Her stomach lurched when she recognized it as the loose floorboard just outside her bedroom door.

The clock by her bedside revealed it was nearly one in the morning. Ever since it had started, she hadn't slept a night through. She usually woke up at the time of night Uncle Harris was most restless—just after midnight or a bit later. Since that was usually the time of his visits, her body had entered fight or flight mode, and as a result, woke her up around twelve-fifteen each night.

He hadn't come to her in about a month. Tammy had been safe, as well.

The creak outside her door made her heart thump hard against her chest as her entire body tingled with palpable fear and she grit her teeth, frozen in place, unable to move.

She wondered if she'd imagined it.

But a split second later, she knew she hadn't. The door opened slowly, and a dim ray of light entered first—followed by the considerable girth of Uncle Harris, who carefully shut the door behind him.

She saw him wobble on his feet and knew he was drunk. He wouldn't have come here if he wasn't. When he was sober, he was a different person, and Clara's panicked psyche had long since begun separating the two men in her mind—the sober Harris and the drunk one—carefully compartmentalizing each trait of their personalities, turning them into two very different people.

It was the only way she could live in the same house with Uncle Harris.

There was no doubt about it—there existed a Harris she could trust, and one she couldn't.

The worst of the two slowly advanced on her bed as she pretended to sleep, her eyes half-open so she could keep an eye on his movements like a deer hiding in the underbrush from a hunter.

Sometimes, if she stayed still, he would just watch her sleep for a while before leaving.

She wasn't so lucky this time.

His heavy body pressed into the mattress as he sat. Then he whispered in a low voice, so only she could hear.

"Part of the reason my goddamn brother moved to Florida was 'cuz he thought he could fix somethin'. Braden always thought he could fuckin' fix somethin'."

Uncle Harris's voice slurred, and liquid sloshed in the bottle as he took another gulp. Clara remained perfectly still, wondering where he was going with this.

"When they had you, precious little Clara, Braden and Lynette decided they…they wanted to…to make everything…the *world* better for you. So they got involved in education reform. And that led them to taking jobs at that…at that fuckin' school where they were filled full o' bullets."

He remained silent for a long moment. Clara could feel her pulse pounding in her neck. A cold sweat covered her brow and she resisted the urge to wipe it away. Uncle Harris grumbled under his breath, then asked in a barely audible tone, "Know what I'm gettin' at, little girl?"

She said nothing.

His next words tore her apart. "It's all *your* goddamn fault they're dead."

When his heavy, calloused hand slipped beneath her nightshirt, she pretended as though she were dead. She left her body, slipping away, going somewhere else.

Now, it didn't matter what happened. She wouldn't feel it, anyway.

Gaven didn't like being around people. They were a waste of his time.

Uncle Daniel didn't like this view, and found it disconcerting whenever Gaven insisted that society was morally bankrupt, with nothing good left in the world.

Even Gaven was beginning to have different thoughts about this.

All due to Clara.

She flummoxed him because she was so different from every other woman he'd met. She didn't seem to think he was strange at all. In fact, his lack of emotional response and general inability to be physically intimate didn't even seem to faze her. He considered their last meeting, when she'd held his hand and put her arms around him, seeming to ignore his reluctance. She was brazen, and she appeared to make decisions based on what *she* wanted, rather than waiting for him to come up with something.

Admirable. She wasn't like the rest.

Suspicious. He couldn't help but wonder if there was more to it.

What was she hiding?

Paranoia was one of the things the drugs treated. Gaven had a history of paranoia, but it wasn't the same every day. Some days, he couldn't care less what went on around him. Other days, it seemed as if there were eyes in the walls; he was being watched, he was *sure* of it. Uncle Daniel was up to something. His mother was planning to hurt him.

He *knew* it.

Then…it would fade.

Today proved a fairly good day. He felt comfortable, at ease. His medications ruled out happiness; for that, he had to drink. The alcohol brought the joy back, balancing it out between his medications. This drove him to drink more—and more, and more. He'd perfected hiding booze to an art form. And he was living above a *bar*.

He hadn't stolen from Uncle Daniel, and he didn't intend to. The man didn't deserve it, and Gaven would never slip into the habit of becoming just as bad as the rest of society. No, he wouldn't give up his morals for nothing more than a bottle of eighty-proof happy-juice. Daniel had been good to Gaven, cooked him breakfast, lunch, dinner, and made sure he had everything he needed without being overbearing.

Though today, Daniel seemed to notice Gaven's intense hurry to leave the breakfast table.

"This is just like last time," Daniel noted. "You were in such a rush. You went for a walk…by the woods, you said?"

"Yeah."

"And you're going back to the same spot?"

"Yeah."

For a moment, Gaven and Daniel locked gazes. He could see himself in his uncle; they resembled each other, except for the fact that Gaven had deep brown eyes and Daniel had blue ones. Other than that, his uncle could have been an older version of himself.

"You make a friend or somethin', Gav?"

Gaven's face remained expressionless. "No. Why?"

"I just thought you might have. I mean, maybe you met somebody. I don't know."

"I didn't meet anybody." He stood from the table, carefully wiping his hands on a napkin before setting it beside his plate. "I'll be back later."

"Okay, Gav. Have a good time."

Despite his uncle's obvious suspicion, he didn't pry further.

Gaven was beginning to like Clearwater. There wasn't much around, which meant there weren't many people. It wasn't like West Palm Beach, where there were thousands of people and very few—if any—Gaven could relate to.

He was amazed he'd been shuffled off to this tiny town only to find a woman he connected with. A woman who, amazingly, also came from Florida. What were the chances?

It neared midday. He hurried down the road toward Winterbloom, then took a hard right before walking fast toward the tree line. He was growing accustomed to the winding path, and he stepped carefully around shrubs and trees with ease.

When he reached the half-broken wall, he didn't see her at first. Then he looked down and there she was—curled up, asleep on the moss.

For a moment, he appreciated how small and fragile she looked, with her hands tucked beneath her chin and her hair splayed out behind her. Then, he said aloud, "Clara."

Her eyes snapped open immediately, as if she'd been waiting for him.

She turned her head to look up at him. "Gaven." She reached out. "Help me up, please?"

He took her hand, warm to the touch, and gently tugged her to her feet. She brushed off her jeans in a methodical manner that made him think she wasn't completely present. Her body was there, but her mind lay elsewhere, her gaze distant.

"Are you all right?" he asked. He knew that somewhere in his psyche, he retained the capacity to *feel*, and he wished he could find it. He still cared, even if the sensation couldn't penetrate as deeply as he wished.

She stared at him for a moment and said nothing.

"Something happened." The words left his lips edged with a sense of certainty. "You're hurt." He cocked his head. "You *look* fine, but you aren't. You've been hurt."

They stood close; the only thing between them the stone wall. She slumped forward, suddenly wrapping her small hands around the cloth of his t-shirt.

"Gaven." The tone of her voice betrayed the fact that something inside her had snapped. She pulled him to her, wrapping her arms around him, and he reciprocated. "Oh, Gaven, you have no idea how bad it is."

"Then leave. Come with me."

"I can't."

Somewhat frustrated by her reply, he only stood there, not sure what to do or say next. Everything about the situation made him uncomfortable— what was happening to Clara, and his growing attachment to her. He'd once had the capacity to feel deeply, and it had cost him. Now, every sensation was dulled, but not enough to suppress his feelings for her.

"He came to my room last night." She spoke the words in one breath, as though trying to keep from crying.

"What happened?"

"He…he touched me. It hasn't happened in a month, maybe…but this time…this t-t-time was d-d-d-different."

"How?"

She withdrew from him slightly, and he kept his hands on her forearms, holding her steady. He watched her eyes squeeze shut. Finally, she spoke.

"He told me…he t-t-told me it was all m-m-my fault."

"What was?"

"My parents being killed."

"How could it be your fault? You were six."

"I know, but…Uncle Harris thinks I was what p-p-prompted them to get into e-e-education reform."

"So?"

"So he thinks they wouldn't h-h-have ended up in that s-s-s-situation if it weren't for me. So…so it's my fault."

He didn't know how to convince her it wasn't.

"Clara, he's trying to control you and Tammy. He feels he's lost control of his own life, and you and your cousin are the only things he thinks he can effectively control. Don't you see that? Your parents dying isn't your fault, but your uncle would prefer you believe that so he can keep you under his thumb." When she said nothing, he added, "Please come with me."

He didn't have to ask again. She took his hand, and climbed over the wall.

Chapter Twenty

As Clara walked beside him, he put his arm around her and said, "From what I understand, girls like this stuff."

"What stuff?" She wiped tears from her face with the back of her hand.

"What I'm doing, my arm around you."

"You started it," she teased, tucking herself against him as they walked.

"True."

"So, what are we going to do when we get to your uncle's place?"

"I don't know. I haven't figured that out yet."

She wanted to stop him, grab him and look him in the eyes, remind him of how terrified she was. But they were on a public street, and this was a small town. People would talk.

"Don't worry," he continued. "Uncle Daniel will help us. I know he will."

"Us? Gaven, I'm the one in trouble here."

"And I'm helping you. That means *us*."

Unable to find suitable words to express her relief that he was on her side, she could only mutter, "Thank you."

"Don't thank me. I like you, Clara. I want to help you."

"I just don't see how you can." Her voice broke, and terror thrummed through every cell in her body.

"We'll figure it out. Look, we're almost there." He gestured into the distance, where the squat brick building stood.

Maybe he was right. Maybe she could get help, after all.

When she moved toward the front of the bar, Gaven shook his head. "No, this way. We'll go up the back entrance. It leads into the apartment." Heading around back, he opened the door and led her into a tiny hallway, then up the steps to the apartment.

Once inside, they heard a voice call out. "Gav, is that you?"

"Yeah, Uncle Daniel." He shut the door behind Clara, and led her down another short hallway. "I brought someone to meet you."

"Ah, I see."

Upon turning the corner and facing the small kitchen, they found Uncle Daniel standing at the counter taking cookies off a baking sheet. When he reached behind him to untie the apron that hung over his t-shirt and faded jeans, Clara caught sight of the words scrawled across the front: *Cooking is a man's job, ladies!*

He hung the apron on a hook behind him. The knowing twinkle in his eye was unmistakable as his lips turned up in a grin. "Clara. So good to see you again."

She crossed her arms over her chest instinctively, sticking close to Gaven.

Daniel started to extend his hand in greeting, but then he stopped, fidgeting for a moment as if unsure what to say or do. "Everything all right?" he asked, his brow crinkling.

Clara looked at Gaven, cocking her head. "Does perceptiveness run in your family?"

A small smirk crossed his face before he nodded in Daniel's direction. "Clara needs help. We have to talk."

"Hmm. I see." Daniel turned back to the counter, placing freshly baked cookies into a jar. He took a plate out of the cupboard, piled it with cookies, then grabbed three clean mugs from the dishwasher. "In that case, let's have a seat at the table, drink some coffee, have a snack, and get to know each other. How's that sound?"

When he turned and smiled at her, Clara saw the concern in his eyes. She nodded and followed Gaven to the table. They sat down beside each other, and Daniel took the seat across from them. The apartment was very comfortable, and she felt welcome. But the fear continued to bubble inside her, eating away at her. She kept glancing at the clock, wondering if Uncle Harris would find out she'd left. Did he know about the broken wall?

Daniel followed her gaze to the clock behind him. "You have to head out soon?"

"No," she mumbled. "I j-j-just…"

Gaven reached over and squeezed her hand. "Clara, tell him everything you told me. He can help."

She turned her head and looked at him, tears brimming in her eyes. "How?"

"Give it a shot, kid." Daniel poured coffee into the empty mugs using the carafe he'd placed in the center of the table. "Whatever it is, I'll do my best to help. Any friend of Gaven's is a friend of mine."

She thought of Tammy; her cousin wouldn't have been able to say a word about what went on in that house. But Clara was an outsider. Even though it had been fleeting, she'd had parents who loved her. They were gone now, but she knew what that felt like. She knew life could be better than what she had. And she knew Uncle Harris was sick, his illness taking over everything he did. Making him worse. Making him hurt her.

Without that knowledge, she might've kept her mouth shut.

As it was, she could talk; she could tell Daniel everything even though she'd just met him. Her desperation to escape the Pendleton house increased. She had to get out of there. Maybe she'd finally found a way.

Chapter Twenty-One

She didn't have to say much for Daniel to understand what was going on. For a long time, he sat staring into his coffee as if it would offer some answers. When no counsel was forthcoming, he pushed the mug aside and bit into a cookie, chewing it slowly, seeming to ponder the situation.

"Clara, I…I don't know what to say. I knew something was wrong when I first met you." He finished his cookie and brushed off his hands. "These cookies taste like cardboard all of a sudden. I just…I can't imagine what you've been going through. Losing your parents at such a young age, and now…" He shook his head, his hands in his lap. "I will do anything I can to help you."

"Tha-thank you," she muttered, before reaching out for Gaven's hand.

Daniel leaned forward on the table, crossing his arms in front of him. "Now, Clara, I *do* want to help you, but I hope you realize what this involves." When she didn't answer, he continued. "I'm going to have to call Sheriff Ryder."

"Oh, no." Clara's voice was soft at first, then firm. "Can't I just…maybe I can…" She shook her head, her entire body trembling, before she tugged her hand away from Gaven and wrapped her arms around herself, rocking slowly backward and forward. "Oh God, oh God…" She shook her head, tears streaming down her face. Within seconds, Daniel was kneeling beside her, tugging her hands into his own.

"Hey, kid, it'll be okay. I know it doesn't seem that way now." His face reddened, as if he barely believed the words he was saying. "Look, we can get to the bottom of this. We can get you out of there. But we can't do it without Sheriff Ryder's help. You must understand that."

"I...I...I didn't t-t-tell you about Uncle Harris. W-w-what he does."

"What do you mean?"

Clara lost control, weeping, her whole body shaking with wracking sobs. When she couldn't answer, Gaven explained, "He's a councilman in the next county over. And he's a retired state representative. Clara thinks he's got enough connections that he can't be touched."

"He w-w-won't let me go," she sobbed, "I just know it. And what about Tammy?"

"Her cousin," Gaven said.

"You mean you have a cousin, his daughter, who...is this happening to her, too?" Daniel asked, sounding as if he might be sick. When Clara nodded, Daniel stood and reached for his cell phone. "I'm calling the sheriff. We need help." He looked at her, his piercing gaze reflecting her fear. "Don't you worry about a thing, kid. I'm gonna make sure you're safe."

Ryan sat at his desk and threw his feet up on the scratched surface. Not much was going on today in Clearwater. There'd been a mild dispute in front of the beauty parlor, and he'd had to break up a fight between two women arguing over something to do with a local fundraiser being organized by the women's club. He didn't understand half of it. He leaned back in his chair and sipped the coffee Jennifer had made him when he'd stopped by the café.

Just as he was beginning to think he'd have a moment to relax away from town gossip, the desk phone buzzed. Throwing his feet back on the floor, he grabbed the receiver.

"Yes."

"Sheriff, there's a call for you. Daniel Bridge. Says it's urgent."

"Fine. I'll take the call." He waited a moment, then pressed the blinking button on the phone. "Sheriff Ryan Ryder here."

"Sheriff, this is Daniel Bridge over at On the Rocks. I need you to come to the bar."

Ryan smirked despite himself. "I don't drink during working hours, Mr. Bridge."

"It's not that." There was some shuffling, and Ryan thought he heard a door shutting in the background. Daniel continued, "I have a young lady here at my apartment, a friend of my nephew's, and she's in big trouble. She needs to be protected."

"Why? I don't understand. What's the situation?"

"Sheriff, I'd rather explain this in person. Please, if you could come over to my apartment above the bar, I'd really appreciate it."

"All right. I'll be there in a few minutes."

"Thank you, Sheriff."

When he hung up the phone, he took a long drink of his coffee. He was going to need it.

It didn't take long to reach the bar. Ryan parked his SUV by the back entrance, next to Daniel's Subaru Outback. After slamming the heavy door, he headed into the building and up the back steps, running a hand over the stubble on his chin. Whatever was going on, it sounded critical.

After Daniel ushered him into the apartment, he saw a young couple seated at a dining table. He thought of Jennifer's call, and how she'd described a couple of kids she'd never seen before. These two seemed to fit her description. Without having to ask, he assumed the boy was the nephew Daniel had mentioned on the phone. The girl—a different story.

Something strange was going on; he could feel it.

"Coffee, Sheriff?"

"No, thanks. Just finished a tall one. I'd like to get down to business, if that's all right with you."

"Certainly, have a seat." Daniel sat down, gesturing to the spot beside him at the table.

In seconds, Ryan took in the girl's diminutive appearance, the way she sat slouched close to the boy, her hands in her lap, her face puffy from crying. She was still, so still he might've thought she was some kind of mannequin—until she glanced up, meeting his gaze before looking back down again.

"Sheriff, this is my nephew, Gaven, and his friend, Clara."

"Good to meet you both," Ryan said, taking his hat off and placing it in his lap. "So, what's the trouble here?"

Daniel looked to Clara, who didn't seem in any mood to talk. "Clara, would you like me to tell him?"

When she nodded, Daniel leaned close to Ryan and whispered in his ear.

It was the worst thing he'd heard in a long time. His stomach churned at the thought, and Daniel's words would continue to echo in his mind for weeks on end: *She's being sexually abused by her uncle.*

Ryan watched her for a moment before speaking. "Clara, I'm going to need to get a statement from you. Then we can go after this guy. How old are you?"

"I'll be eighteen in t-t-two weeks."

"I see. And what's your uncle's name?"

"Harris Pendleton."

It was like a punch to the gut. This wasn't going to be so easy, after all.

Chapter Twenty-Two

It was the first time she'd spent a night elsewhere since her parents died. With every moment that passed, she grew more anxious, and as the sun began to set, she tapped her foot against the carpeting, then ground her heel on the bottom of the couch, staring fixedly at the fibers below.

Sheriff Ryder had long since left, and she'd had dinner with Daniel and Gaven. Daniel tried to ask her what she might like to do now that she was away from her uncle's house, but she couldn't envision it. All she could think about was Uncle Harris coming to get her, and the thoughts only worsened as the night wore on.

Resigned to spending the night on Daniel's couch, she tossed and turned, unable to get to sleep. She'd never been able to sleep well at Uncle Harris's house, because she was always afraid he was coming to get her.

She still had the same fears, and something told her they wouldn't dissipate for a long time.

That night, all she could see in her mind was Uncle Harris's face, and Tammy's guilt-inducing stare.

"Why did you leave me here?" her cousin asked, over and over, her face ashen.

"I don't know!" Clara shouted, sobbing. "I'm so sorry, so sorry…oh, please forgive me!"

"Clara."

"Tammy, please, I—" She opened her eyes with a start and realized it was Gaven who'd spoken. He knelt beside the couch, holding her hand. A bit of light snuck in between the blinds covering the windows. "Gaven." Her voice strained, her throat sore, she rubbed her eyes and sat up. "What…what happened?"

"You were crying out in your sleep." He nodded toward the windows. "It's a little past six in the morning."

"Oh God." She gasped, her heart pounding, her skin clammy as she tugged her hand away from his. "Uncle Harris, he'll know…oh, Gaven, he knows I'm gone now. What…what'll I do?"

"It's okay." His expression looked blank, but his eyes betrayed a hint of concern. "Uncle Daniel's making a couple calls now. Sheriff Ryder didn't want us to know last night, but he said we need to get you somewhere safe…somewhere even the sheriff doesn't know about."

"What do you mean?"

"If Sheriff Ryder doesn't know where you are, he won't have to lie to your uncle. So, we're going to hide you someplace until he can figure out what to do next."

"Oh." Clara tugged the blanket off her body and planted her feet on the floor. "You mean, he doesn't want to lie, so he's making it so he doesn't have to?"

"Exactly." Gaven sat down beside her just as there was a shuffling in the next room, and the sound of a bedroom door opening.

Daniel emerged clad in jeans and a t-shirt, his hair moist from a recent shower. "Good morning, Clara," he said, seemingly unsure of his words. After all, how could it possibly be a *good* morning?

"Hi, Dan." She rose, still wearing yesterday's clothes, and ran her hand through her messy hair. "What's the plan?"

"I just got off the phone with a couple people. Called some friends of mine, but they couldn't help out. I didn't give them much information, just that I had a friend who needed somewhere to stay. Then I called Chloe over at Winterbloom, and she said yes. Now, I know—"

Before he could console her, she shook her head adamantly. "No, no, I can't…that's right near Uncle Harris's. I can't stay there."

"Hold on." He raised his hands in the air. "Just a second. After Chloe pried a little, I told her the whole story. Not everybody knows the Pendletons live so close, but Chloe did. A friend of hers at the White House used to work with your uncle. Chloe was shocked about what's been happening, that's for sure, but she thinks Winterbloom is the best place for you. Your uncle would never suspect you'd be hiding so close, especially since Winterbloom is a bed and breakfast. Since you don't have any money, he'd never expect you to be there."

"I *don't* have any money, I can't pay her…"

"That's okay." Daniel stepped across the room, tentatively placing his hand on her shoulder in an attempt to soothe her. "Chloe said she and her husband, Jordan, will let you stay there for free for a little while if you're willing to help out around the place. The building is pretty well hidden from the road, so are the cabins, but if you're worried about being seen, she said she's got plenty to keep you busy in the house. What do you think?"

"I...I guess so." Her mind reeled; she'd only just left her uncle's home, and she was *staying* away. She didn't want to go back there, but she was terrified for Tammy. What would her cousin do without her?

"You look so unsure." Daniel withdrew his hand, frowning. "You're going to be okay, Clara."

"I know...I mean, I think I know. But...what about my cousin? What about Tammy?"

Daniel and Gaven exchanged a worrisome glance.

"We'll figure out a way to get her out of there, too," Daniel promised. "Ready to go to Winterbloom? I'd feed you breakfast, but I think it's best to get you out of here."

"Yes, Gaven mentioned what the sheriff said. I'm...shocked by that. It's too kind of him."

"Sheriff Ryder is a good man." Daniel grabbed his keys from the kitchen counter and emerged, slipping his sunglasses over his eyes. "Come on, kids. Clara, I'm going to ask that you sit in the back seat and stay hidden from view. We can't let anyone see you."

"What about...what about my clothes, what am I going to wear when I'm there?" She shrugged, indicating everything she had was on her person.

Daniel smirked. "Don't worry. Knowing Chloe, she'll take care of everything."

Chapter Twenty-Three

It was a gorgeous summer day. To Chloe, it didn't matter that it was Monday. The days tended to meld together because she enjoyed her work so much; Winterbloom Bed and Breakfast was her life, made even better because she had someone to share it with.

She did a few things around the house, then cleaned up the kitchen since the innkeeper, Hope, had gone away for a few days. Then she stood at the window and stared out toward the log home Jordan had built for them— the perfect place in which to raise their beautiful daughter, Bianca.

But something didn't feel right. A darkness had clouded her morning, and it was barely six-thirty. She pulled her long, curly red hair into a messy ponytail and sighed, tucking her hands into the pockets of her jeans.

"What's up with you, sweetheart?"

Heavy footsteps behind her announced the presence of her husband. She couldn't help but smile as he wrapped his arms around her. With a start, she turned and nearly whacked her head against his chin. "Bianca?"

"Relax. She's fast asleep. I just came over to grab a couple tools I left in the basement, then I'm heading back to put the finishing touches on that bookshelf in the den. I'll keep an eye on our little angel." He kissed her on the cheek. "You nearly took me out, you moved so quick," he added, chuckling.

"Sorry. You know how I get."

"I know. You look like you're lost in thought."

"I am. Someone's coming to stay for a while."

"So? People come to stay here all the time."

"No, not like that."

"What, a boarder?"

She turned in his arms, reaching up to caress his cheek and run her hand through his shortly cropped hair. "A teenager who's in some trouble. Daniel just called."

"What do you mean? What kind of trouble?"

When Chloe told him what had happened to the girl, who her uncle was, and what the man had done for a living, Jordan's eyes widened. All he could say was, "Holy shit."

Chloe stepped out of his arms when she heard the doorbell ring. "You can say that again, baby. Looks like our *boarder* is here."

Old trees with heavy branches and thick foliage, standing tall on the crest of a hill, had shielded Clara from the road when she climbed out of Daniel's Subaru.

She hadn't showered since yesterday morning, and the discomfort of wearing yesterday's clothes was quickly wearing on her. Other than shopping trips with Aunt Nan, she'd never left the property, so she wasn't accustomed to the things other girls her age saw as commonplace—parties, sleepovers, hanging out with friends. She figured this must be how foreigners felt when they traveled to America for the first time, taking in the sights, scents, and customs of a culture so unlike their own.

Clara knew she'd slip behind in her studies; she'd left her books at home, thinking she'd be back. Aunt Nan always helped her with mathematics on Monday mornings, even during the summer, joking it was *math Monday*. But today was the start of a strange new life, and there was no way she could go back. Even if she did return to Uncle Harris's house, he'd keep her on an even shorter leash.

I don't want to go back.

"This way, Clara."

She took Gaven's hand, drawn to him, knowing he was her anchor in an uncharted sea.

The beauty of Winterbloom was breathtaking, an old house on a hill with a wide, inviting front porch. The short steps leading to the front door were firm beneath her feet, the wood appeared freshly painted.

Daniel seemed to notice her trepidation as she realized she was shaking with every breath.

"It'll be okay, Clara," he assured her, but she sensed the doubt in his voice. People in high places could get away with things; she had read enough to know it was true.

When they rang the doorbell, it didn't take long before the wide, heavy door opened and a beautiful woman with red hair and a face dotted with freckles answered the door. She stepped aside, ushering them in.

"Welcome. You must be Clara."

Her voice was soft, filled with sympathy and a deep sense of *knowing*. She'd been told all about her, and this worried Clara. How many people knew? Daniel said he hadn't told anyone except Chloe the full story, but could she trust him?

As if sensing her uncertainty, Chloe opened her arms, leading them into the cozy sitting room off the main entrance. "Please, don't be frightened. Daniel told me everything, but I'm here to help. Winterbloom Bed and Breakfast has a nice assortment of rooms, and you're welcome to any one of them you'd like, though we might have to rearrange things when the season starts." She glanced toward Daniel, then back at Clara. "All I need is a little help around the house. Our innkeeper, Hope, can show you the ropes when she returns from visiting her friends."

"But…but you d-d-don't even know me. Why would you…"

"Clara, I think you'll find the citizens of Clearwater are very much like a big family. This town has its issues just like anywhere else, and there've been plenty of times when people haven't gotten along, but all in all, we're a friendly bunch. Speaking for myself, my grandmother taught me how important it is to be there for those in need." She paused for a moment. "How old are you?"

"Seventeen." Stammering, she added, "I'll be…I mean, I'm going to be eighteen in a couple weeks."

"Please, have a seat." After Chloe leaned back on a loveseat, everyone else made themselves comfortable.

Clara sank into an antique armchair just as a big man entered the room, running his hand over the stubble on his cheek.

"Daniel, you've met my husband." Chloe patted the cushion beside her, and the tall, military man plopped down beside her, taking her hand.

"Jordan, this is Daniel's nephew from Florida, Gaven, and this is his friend, Clara."

"Good to meet you both," Jordan intoned. Smiling warmly at Clara, he added, "You're more than welcome to stay here."

Clara's discomfort must have been fairly obvious; she realized she'd been holding her breath until Jordan spoke. Digging her fingernails into the seat of the chair, she bit her bottom lip and said, "What if…w-w-what if he…"

"Sheriff Ryder doesn't know you're here. That's the important thing," Chloe interrupted. "He's a good man, but this protects you. I'm sure he'll suspect you're here, but as long as he doesn't know for sure, he won't be able to answer any of your uncle's questions. That gives us a bit of time while we figure out what to do. It's probably best if Gaven doesn't come to see you for a little while, and—"

Clara couldn't stop the words from tumbling out of her mouth. "No, please, I need Gaven." Heat crept into her face as Gaven stepped closer to where she sat. She looked at Chloe as she held back the tears that threatened to fall. "He…I would've never left if…if it w-w-weren't for him. You have to understand, I've never left Uncle Harris's home."

When Gaven placed his hand on her shoulder, it seemed to ground her in the present moment, allowing her to speak. "Somehow, he found me, and we got to talking. I climbed over the broken part of the wall at the back of the estate, and he took me into town. I don't even know why…" Nervous laughter escaped her lips. "I don't know why I trusted him, I just…something about him…"

Chloe's full lips turned up, accentuating the freckles on her cheeks. "I know." She looked at Jordan with adoration in her gaze, then back at Clara. "I have a pretty good idea what you're feeling, Clara, and I definitely understand. But we can't give your uncle any reason to think you've been seeing Gaven, and we don't want Daniel to get in trouble for helping you, either. Just a few days, okay? That should give us the time we need. Sheriff Ryder can get the case together, and I'm sure they can get your uncle behind bars for what he's done."

"No!" Clara found herself shouting. "Tammy...please, you can't. Tammy, my cousin, she'll get hurt!"

A part of her regretted what she'd said when she saw the pained looks on their faces. Chloe's eyes brimmed with tears.

Jordan looked as if he were gritting his teeth. Finally, he broke the silence. "Listen, Clara. You don't know me, but I don't take well to a man who hurts a woman. We'll figure out a way to get your cousin out of there—no matter what. For now, you stay here and lay low. Let us worry about the ways and means, okay?"

Clara met his gaze. His eyes were sharp, and she could tell he was haunted, just as she was. Darkness clouded her vision, the shadows of her memories closing in on her. Somehow, she knew she could trust him. She saw it in his eyes.

"Okay," she said, sounding less confident than she felt. "I'll stay."

Chapter Twenty-Four

Tammy completed her school work in her bedroom, listening to the muffled voices of her parents arguing. The argument migrated into the hall, the voices growing closer, until footsteps pounded down the main staircase and she couldn't hear them anymore.

She set aside her work, picking up her favorite book and clutching it to her chest. *Twenty Thousand Leagues Under the Sea* offered a sense of security she received from nothing and no one else. She held the book as though it were a lifeline as she carefully opened the door and crept out into the long hallway.

Carefully avoiding the creaky spots in the floor, she moved to the top of the steps and froze against the wall. Her mother's voice floated up to her from the den. She'd never heard her mother say such things.

"Harris. Listen to me." Her voice was firm, unyielding. "You've driven the girl away, that's what happened. What would your brother say?"

"My *brother* is dead!" Harris roared. "It's his goddamn fault this happened. Look at what happened to him and Lynette. The same thing could happen to our Tammy. Don't you see that? If we send her to school like you're saying, she could get killed."

"For crying out loud, Harris, it's only a few months until she graduates. Just let her *meet* people. For all you know, the house could catch on fire and we could *all* die."

"You're being irrational. The world is a dangerous place for a young girl."

Stony silence followed. Tammy's heart pounded in her throat as she wondered what her mother was thinking. Did she *know?* Did she have any idea what happened to her daughter behind that bedroom door, what Tammy's father did to her? She must know; after all, if Daddy did those things to her, it was probably just what fathers did. It was normal, wasn't it? Tammy had always been afraid to ask her, worried her mother would think Tammy was trying to ruin her husband. Tammy was a bad girl; whatever she got, she deserved. At least, that was what her father said. On the other hand, he shielded her from the world. From the dangers beyond the front door.

How dangerous was the world, really? That familiar ache passed through her chest, and she wondered what it was like out there. She'd been shopping with her mother in Jackson Hole, and she only knew of Clearwater through conversation. It must be pretty awful if Daddy was so intent on protecting her from it.

"I'm calling Detective Barndt, my old buddy. He can find Clara," her father was saying.

"Harris, she's barely been gone a day! You don't even know when she left yesterday. You know enough to realize you can't get the police on this until after twenty-four hours. And she's nearly eighteen! How do you know she hasn't—"

"What? *Met* someone?" Tammy's father chuckled dryly, but there was no humor in his voice. "How could she meet anybody? She doesn't leave the property."

"Why don't you just ask around? Talk to people in Clearwater. Maybe someone's seen her. You don't need to call Detective Barndt yet, Harris. Be *reasonable*. He doesn't even work in this town."

After a long pause, her father grumbled. "Oh, all right. I'll go to Sheriff Ryder first. He might know something."

"There, now. That makes more sense than anything you've said so far."

As her mother rounded the corner and headed up the steps, Tammy scurried back into her room, hoping she hadn't been seen.

Chapter Twenty-Five

"I *have* to go back." Clara's whisper sounded hoarse, her words forced out by the terrifying desperation that rose with the bile in her stomach. She and Gaven had been given a few moments of private time to talk in the next room, where she squeezed his hands in hers as if worried he might disappear.

"Clara, listen to me." When he drew her close, she watched the way his dark hair slipped over his forehead, the way his eyes focused on her, so full of fierce loyalty and knowledge. "You'll be okay here, I'm sure of it. Chloe and Jordan seem like really great people. I'll be back before you know it. We just have to wait until this blows over. Please, *don't* go back there."

"What about Tammy?"

"You heard them. We'll make sure she's safe, too. You just have to give it time."

She found solace when she was close to him, so she leaned her head against his chest, shut her eyes, and listened to his heartbeat.

For a long moment, they were both quiet until Gaven spoke.

"Why do you like me?"

She turned her head, looking up at him. "What do you mean?"

"I mean exactly what I asked. Why are you interested in me? You have to realize I'm not like other people. I can't…Clara, I don't *feel* things like other people. This medication dulls it. It makes me crazy. The only time I feel anything is when I drink. I'm a goddamn child in a man's body, don't you see?" He stared into her eyes, leaning his forehead against hers. "You need to be with someone you can really depend on. Not me."

"No, Gaven. Don't say things like that." She turned her head up slightly so she could look straight into his eyes. The sensation coursing through her, heat rushing through her body, made her dizzy with desire. It was so unfamiliar to her; she welcomed it, for his company had become something she refused to relinquish. "Gaven, I don't want anyone else." She made sure he could see into her eyes, see the truth in her gaze as she spoke. "I love you."

He wrapped his arms around her and held her for a long time. She craved his warmth and closeness; she didn't want him to leave. But he had to. He gently withdrew from her arms, running his hands down along her shoulders.

"Clara, sometimes I don't know what's going on inside me. And I'm not sure you'd like who I am if you really got to know me."

"Gaven, that's not—"

"Let me finish. Maybe you won't like all of me. Sometimes, I'm not very pleasant to be around. But…" He held her hands in his, gently squeezing them.

"But what, Gaven?"

"I love you, too, Clara."

Her heart overflowed with relief now that she knew the truth, quickly followed by sorrow because she was so afraid she wouldn't see him again. After all she'd been through, after all the heartache she'd experienced in her young life, she didn't want to lose him. She'd fallen in love in just a few short days, and they'd been the best times of her life, despite being shadowed by the pain and terror awaiting her at home. Maybe he thought he wasn't normal, or that he was broken somehow, but to her, he was perfect with all his flaws and idiosyncrasies. She wouldn't have him any other way.

"You'll come back, right?" Her words were barely a whisper.

"Of course."

At first, he appeared uncertain, and he moved robotically as if he didn't know quite what to do. It was with hesitant movements that he leaned forward and pressed his lips against hers. He held them there for several long seconds, and she relished in the sensation of the kiss. With gentle encouragement, she brushed her lips against his, moving them softly and making the moment even more wonderful.

It ended all too quickly.

"Gaven, time to go," Daniel called from the other room.

He withdrew slowly, placing his hand tentatively against her cheek, caressing her with an awkwardness that made her think yet again that he might've read about this sort of thing in books, but never completely experienced it until now. Just like her.

"I have to go," he whispered.

"I know. But…come back to me, okay?"

"I will. I promise."

She could see the certainty in his eyes and knew nothing would keep him from returning to her. Both of them feared being hurt. But they both knew, deep down, that neither would betray the other. They could *trust* each other. And that was something they each needed more than anything else.

Chapter Twenty-Six

Ryan was expecting company, but not so soon. Having finished up his paperwork for the morning, he was about to leave the office when the phone buzzed.

"Yes?"

"Sheriff, Harris Pendleton is here to see you."

"Ah. Send him right in."

He hung up the phone and sat back down in his chair, leaning against the desk. A moment later, a big, burly man in black dress slacks, a white shirt, and a sport jacket entered the room. His brown hair was cropped short, and he looked very much like the photograph Ryan had seen of him some years back, when he was reading up on local politics. Despite his knowledge of the man who stood before him, Ryan pretended he had no idea who he was.

"Sir, what can I do for you?" He rose from his seat, extending his hand.

"Harris Pendleton. You must be Sheriff Ryder."

The man's handshake was firm, his skin cool to the touch. Withdrawing, Ryan indicated the chair across from his desk. "Have a seat, Mr. Pendleton. What can I help you with today?"

"My niece, Clara Pendleton, is missing." He lowered his heavy frame into the leather-cushioned chair. "I need your help locating her." When he fixed the sheriff with an intimidating stare, Ryan could tell how this man had gotten things done during his days as a politician. He had clout, he had power, and Ryan was just a small town sheriff; it was quite possible the man could crush him like an insect.

"Well." He cleared his throat, pulling out his notepad. "How long has she been missing?"

"She disappeared sometime yesterday."

He met the man's gaze. "I'm afraid that's not enough time. We won't be able to file a missing person report."

"I'm aware of that. This is a small town. You wouldn't happen to know where she is, would you?"

"I'm sorry, no. It *is* a small town, but that doesn't mean I know everyone." He paused, adding, "I don't know where your niece is, Mr. Pendleton."

"Sheriff, do you know who I am?"

Ryan made a show of scratching his chin and shaking his head slowly. "Hmm, I'm afraid I'm not familiar with your background. Should I be?"

"I am a retired state representative, Sheriff Ryder. I have connections in this state, and elsewhere. My family has lived in Clearwater for six generations. The Pendletons have donated funds over the years to help the town, the schools, the historical society. Understand, Sheriff, my niece is important to me. My *family* is important to me. Therefore, I expect you to report to me if you see my niece, or if anyone you know sees her." He took a photo from the pocket of his sport jacket and dropped it on the ink blotter in front of Sheriff Ryder, along with a business card. "I apologize for being so brusque, but you understand my position."

"Of course, Mr. Pendleton."

The man rose from the seat, shaking Ryan's hand again. He smiled, not unkindly, adding, "Call me Harris."

"Certainly. We'll be in touch, Harris."

When he left his office, shutting the door behind him, Ryan released a heavy breath and slumped into his office chair.

He felt as if he'd lost every ounce of energy in him.

Over the next few days, Clara learned every crevice of Winterbloom. When Hope returned from vacation, she was happy to meet her, accepting the extra help without question. Chloe asked for her sizes, and brought her several outfits one day, which touched her heart and made her feel more at home at the bed and breakfast.

At night, she was alone in the old house since Chloe, Jordan, and their daughter lived behind the building in their own cabin. It was an eerie feeling, being in a strange new place. She pondered this as she swept around the stairs, lost in thought.

"Hey! What's up, yo?"

Clara startled at the faintly familiar voice, and swung around. She immediately recognized the young girl with her mousy brown hair and olive complexion, clad in a Jimi Hendrix t-shirt, her thumbs in the belt loops of her jean shorts.

"Lisa."

"You remember me!" the girl exclaimed. Her short hair looked windswept, even though it wasn't windy out. She shut the front door behind her and clasped her hands together in apparent excitement. "I can't believe you remember me."

"I *definitely* remember you. How could I forget the girl who gave my aunt a full moon?"

"Aw, shucks, Clara, you're never going to let me live that down, are you?" She spoke as though they were friends and would see a lot of each other. Clara found herself liking the implication. "Well, I just came to see if Chloe needed some extra help cleaning." Lisa eyed the dustpan in Clara's hand. "But it looks like the position might have already been taken."

"Yeah, sorry. I'm the temporary maid. I kinda hope it lasts longer, though," she mumbled.

"Why wouldn't it?"

"It's a long story." She swept a bit of dirt into the dustpan and dumped it into a nearby trash receptacle. "Family stuff. My uncle's a little crazy. He…he might not let me keep the job," she hazarded.

"It's okay, I know how you feel." Lisa shrugged, her body language revealing her openness. "My dad was kinda wacky; that's why my mom divorced him. He used to hit her. So, I totally get it. If your uncle is anything like that, I know what you mean."

Clara met Lisa's gaze. "My uncle is *worse* than that, if you can believe it."

"Shit."

"Yeah." Clara popped open the small closet door behind her and put away the broom and dustpan.

"Don't worry." Lisa reached out, brushing a hand against Clara's arm. "I totally get it."

Smiling at Lisa, she gestured toward the kitchen. "Cup of tea, coffee?" She'd already learned to help herself; Chloe didn't mind.

"Sure."

As Lisa followed her into the kitchen, a warmth passed through Clara as she realized she'd made a friend.

Finally.

Chapter Twenty-Seven

Ryan climbed the steps up to the front door of Dave Johnson's law practice, which was housed in one of the oldest buildings in Clearwater. Turning the antique knob, he stepped inside to be greeted by the chill of the air-conditioned front room.

Dave's secretary sat at the front desk wearing a heavy sweater.

"Ah, Alessandra, I see Dave is fantasizing about sub-zero temperatures again," he said.

"Oh, yes." Her shoulder-length brown hair fell free about her neck; she usually had it in a bun, but maybe she was hoping it would keep her from catching a chill. "You can go in, Sheriff. When you do, make a show of shivering. Maybe he'll turn the air up so I can thaw out."

"All right, I'll see what I can do." He winked at her, and she seemed to melt a little; maybe that would help a bit.

In the office, Dave sat behind his desk clad in a blue suit, an iPad in hand as he flicked his finger across the screen. He glanced up when Ryan entered.

"Oh, hey, Sheriff! Come on in." He popped forward in his chair, gesturing to the empty seat across from his desk.

Ryan plopped down on the soft cushion. "Hey, Dave, how've you been?"

"Oh, fine…nothing too crazy to report. It's too damn hot, though."

"It's only eighty degrees outside."

"Like I said, too damn hot."

"Well, you're turning your poor secretary into an icicle out there," he joked.

"Aw, she complains about air conditioning no matter how cool it is."

"I heard that!" a muffled voice from the other room called out.

Dave shook his head. "You know, when I bought this place, the previous owner implied the walls were thick. But Alessandra can hear me whenever I'm on the phone, and I can hear her. 'Course, when you think about it, it makes things a little easier. I never have to tell her anything; she already knows." He laughed. "How've things been for you, Ryan?"

"Fine, for the most part. Easy day. That's why I love being a cop in Clearwater. It's not as wild as the big city I used to work in." He paused, chuckling. "Like yesterday, got a call from Mrs. Willard. She's got a new neighbor. I had to go out there because Mrs. Willard didn't like where the new neighbor parked, on the street in front of her house."

"But doesn't Mrs. Willard live in a duplex?"

"Yep. The neighbor in the other side of the duplex had to park there because her uncle had to park his pick-up truck on the street, too. There wasn't room anywhere else. I had a hell of a time trying to reason with her."

"Well, Mrs. Willard's been kinda nutty ever since her husband passed."

"That's the truth."

"Coffee, tea?" Dave rose and went to a small station in the corner, retrieving two mugs.

"Coffee will be fine, thank you."

"So, what brings you here?" He filled the mugs, then tossed a few sugar packets in Ryan's direction before handing him a steaming mug of coffee. "Much as I love talking to an old friend about town gossip, I can tell you're on duty."

"Yeah…" Ryan stared into the dark liquid for a moment, as if hoping he'd find answers in it. "I've got kind of a sensitive situation, Dave. I don't like it one bit. I have a real bad feeling."

"How so? Should I put my lawyer hat on, or leave it off?"

"Well, I don't know. Part of the reason I'm here is just to bounce this off a friend, but…"

"Need some legal advice, pal?"

"I have a feeling you won't be able to offer much."

Ryan explained the situation with Clara Pendleton, and Clara's fears regarding her cousin Tammy.

"Hmm, you're right." Dave sipped his coffee, frowning. His salt-and-pepper made him look distinguished, but as he sat there thinking through the problem, he looked a lot older.

Knowledge could age a man, and so could memories. Ryan knew that better than anyone.

"Social Services, you think?" Ryan asked.

"Yes. Yes, I think that's your best approach. Get Social Services involved, get them to the house. The only thing is, if this cousin…"

"Tammy."

"If Tammy's tight-lipped about it, they're not going to be able to do anything. Everything could look innocent as daises in the broad light of day."

"Don't I know it."

"How old is Clara?"

"She'll be eighteen soon. If I'm not mistaken, in a little over a week."

"That's good. She'll be able to help her cousin more once she's legally an adult." Dave leaned over the desk, adding, "Let me tell you what little I know about this kind of situation…"

"I'm glad you stopped by," Clara said, though she felt her cheeks warm with embarrassment. She wasn't accustomed to talking to anyone other than Tammy, least of all someone her own age.

"For sure. I need to make some extra money, so let me know if you hear anything. You go to the Clearwater School? I never saw you there before. Well, not that I lasted long there, anyway," Lisa said as she sat at the table in the kitchen with Clara. The afternoon sun played through the beaded decorations in the wide windows, sending rainbows and glimmers across the white tiles and the wood of the table.

Clara held her mug as though it were a lifeline. "Uh, I don't go to school. I mean, I'm homeschooled…well, not anymore. I was almost done with high school."

"Oh, you got a lot of drama goin' on, right?"

"That's an understatement."

They were both quiet for a long moment, as Lisa seemed to be wondering what Clara was hiding. Thankfully, she didn't ask. She rambled on about her mother, her parents' divorce, and a guy she had a crush on. Surprising Clara, she reached across the table and laid her hand on hers. "You know, if you ever want to vent or anything, I'm here. Whatever you tell me, it'll be between us."

"Thank you," she said gratefully, fidgeting in her seat. "I'll be here, if you want to come hang out sometime. I'm living here now."

"Cool, I will." After finishing the last of her tea, Lisa rose from her seat.

Clara showed her to the door, and Lisa departed in a whirlwind of energy, throwing her bag over her shoulder and running along the driveway under the oak trees.

As she shut the door, she wondered what it must be like to be normal like that. To have a regular childhood. She'd had a normal life until she was six, and then it was taken away from her.

"I guess I'll never know," she muttered as she returned to her duties.

Chapter Twenty-Eight

After dinner, Bianca went right to sleep and Chloe headed into the living room, plopping down on the couch with Jordan. Her husband immediately muted the television and turned to look at her, slipping his hand around hers.

"How's our boarder?" he asked, his eyes showing sympathy.

"You've been real worried about her, haven't you?" She tilted her head, kissing him on the cheek.

"Of course. I know you're worried, too."

"But with you it's different," she noted. "You've been through hell, and so has she. You have something in common. We all have our share of secrets and pain, but you've got enough for ten men."

"I know what it's like to live through trauma. I know how hard it can be."

"Well, she seems to be doing all right, but…"

"But?"

"Last night…" Chloe heaved a sigh. "I headed back to the house to do some last minute things, and when I was upstairs putting some sheets away in the linen closet, I heard loud sobbing. She'd left the door to her room open a little bit. I stepped in and started to ask if she was okay, and then I realized she was asleep. So, I sat down on the edge of the bed and just...gently woke her up." Chloe was conscious of tears welling in her eyes. She rubbed them with the back of her hand. "I didn't want to scare her...but she did seem confused at first to see me. We talked for a couple minutes. She's been having terrible nightmares, but she said she didn't realize she talked in her sleep."

She stared for a moment at the harsh light of the television, watching people speak without any sound. It was like Clara, whose screams had been muted until she left her uncle's house. "Oh, Jordan. I just wish I could help her more."

He squeezed her thigh, soothing her. "I think it's time we call together the troops."

"What do you mean?"

"Well, I could talk to her a bit. Give her my side of things, tell her how I've been working through my past. And I can call Gioven, too, now that he's decided to stay in Clearwater."

Chloe had once been very wary of Sergeant Gioven Sparks, a Marine who'd seen more than his fair share of horrors, but now that he'd turned away from the bottle and made friends with some of the locals, he'd shown a more sensitive side of himself few had seen before.

As a former Gunnery Sergeant in the Marines, Jordan had returned to civilian life with post traumatic stress disorder. He and Chloe both knew PTSD could come from any trauma, and perhaps he was right. Maybe he and Gioven could offer some consolation to the girl.

"But don't forget it was a man who did those things to her. I should be with you when you talk to her."

"I agree. At least, she's got one thing on her side. She's almost eighteen, and he won't be able to lay any claim on her then."

"Oh, Jordan!" Chloe exclaimed. "Her birthday, I'd nearly forgotten!"

Jordan smirked. "Party?"

"Exactly. It'll be perfect." She squeezed his hand and jumped from the couch. "I have to start planning. This is going to be great."

"Let me know if you need any help." Jordan un-muted the television as Chloe scurried into the office.

Chapter Twenty-Nine

Gaven nearly spilled his coffee at Express Ohh's when an ear-splitting shriek of joy filled the air and Lisa rushed over to his side.

"Oh my *gawd*, I remember you! You're Clara's boyfriend."

As he watched her cheeks flush in excitement, he wished he could sink into the floor and disappear. The excessiveness of her hyper attitude irritated him, reminding him of why he'd fallen for Clara in the first place—sweet, quiet, sincere Clara.

He backed up a few steps, trying to retain some of his personal space, while he glared in her direction. "Hello, Lisa. I haven't seen Clara, if that's what you were going to ask me."

"I have, she's over at Winterbloom."

This surprised him, and he almost choked as he sipped from the to-go cup in his hand. His gaze darted about at the short line of people who were waiting for their orders before he grabbed Lisa by the arm and practically dragged her from the coffee shop.

"Hey!" Lisa exclaimed, wrenching her arm away from him as they emerged onto the sidewalk. "What gives?"

"Didn't she tell you not to say anything?" Gaven snapped.

"What? No." Lisa threw her head back, looking at him as if he were a freak. Maybe she didn't mean it that way, and maybe she did—but she was looking at him the way those girls in West Palm Beach looked at him.

Steeling himself, he explained. "No one can know she's there, at least not until her eighteenth birthday in a week. She didn't tell you?"

"I just *said* she didn't say anything. Jeez."

"Look, it's not my place to tell you, but she's hiding from her uncle. He can't find out where she is. Do you understand?"

Lisa's brow furrowed and she watched him as if hoping his expression would reveal something more. "Oh. Oops."

"Yeah. So, don't say anything." Gaven glanced through the window of the coffee shop, then back at Lisa. "I don't want anything to happen to Clara."

"Wow." Lisa twirled her iPod in her hand, twisting the wire of her ear buds around her finger. "You really love her, don't you?"

"Yeah. I do." He turned on his heel and walked away, leaving Lisa alone on the sidewalk.

✧✦★✦✧

A guest at Winterbloom had just left, so Clara busied herself cleaning up the room and washing all the linens. Chloe's face was alight with anticipation when she told Clara her friend, a bestselling author named Melissa Edwards, was coming for her usual two-week stay at Winterbloom. She would be there within an hour or so, and it was Clara's job to prepare the room for her.

When she finished, she slumped on the bed and imagined, just for a moment, that she'd grown up in this house. She pictured her mother and father alive and well, raising her here in Clearwater. She wondered if her uncle was right, at least a little bit. If Clara had been the inspiration for her parents' involvement in education reform, and their employment at a school they felt needed more attention than most, then was she partially to blame for their deaths? If Clara had never been born, would they still be alive?

A light knock at the half-open door distracted her from her morose thoughts. She glanced up and saw Chloe, wearing jean shorts, a maroon blouse, and running shoes.

"Hey, hon." Chloe stepped in and sat beside her. "You okay?"

"Yeah, everything's fine. I just finished cleaning up in here." She glanced about, looking for any last-minute things that needed tidying. "I think the room's ready for your friend."

"It looks wonderful, but I was asking how *you* were doing."

"Oh, I'm all right."

Chloe patted her on the leg. "You're not a very good liar, but I'll accept that," she said with a wink. "I think I know something that will cheer you up. Gaven's downstairs."

Clara straightened, her heart rate picking up speed.

"I thought that might bring a glow to your cheeks." Chloe giggled, rising from where she sat. "Come on, I've got a pot of coffee on."

Gaven was standing by the bay window in the sitting room, looking out over the front yard. When Clara stepped into the room, a small smile caused the dimple to appear in his cheek. An indescribable warmth filled her, and she wrapped her arms around him, hugging him close.

"I missed you," she whispered.

"I missed you, too. Daniel thought it was probably okay for me to come by." He stepped back, nodding to the owner of Winterbloom. "Hello, Chloe."

"Would either of you two like some coffee?"

"I'll have some," Clara said, squeezing Gaven's hand.

"None for me, thank you." He frowned. "I've already had coffee today. And I'm sort of regretting it."

"What do you mean?" Clara asked.

As Chloe headed for the kitchen, Gaven sat down on the sofa and patted the cushion beside him. "I just wanted to warn you. I was at Express Ohh's, and your friend, Lisa, found me there. Did you tell her no one could know you're here?"

Clara shook her head, dread rising within her, causing goose bumps to crawl steadily along her arms. "No…I didn't tell her to keep it quiet. I guess I should have."

"Well, she came up to me in the coffee shop and said *out loud* that you were here at Winterbloom." Gaven shook his head, seeming annoyed. "This is a tiny town, and in the short time I've been here, I've already seen how quickly word can travel about anything. I hope your uncle doesn't come looking for you."

Chloe stepped into the room, holding two mugs of coffee. She handed one to Clara. "Uh-oh," she mumbled. "What's up?"

Gaven looked up at her, his face impassive. "Her friend, Lisa, mentioned Clara was here at Winterbloom when she ran into me at Express Ohh's."

"Ah, I see. I'm sure it'll be all right." Chloe sat across from them on the loveseat. "Don't let things like this stop you from making friends, Clara. I'm certain Lisa didn't mean it. She's a little wild, but she's a good kid."

"I guess." Clara sipped her coffee and leaned back. "It won't really matter after next Sunday, anyway."

"That's true." Gaven leaned back into the soft cushions as well. "After next weekend, you'll be *safe*…legally and otherwise."

Chapter Thirty

Having spent way too much time inside, Clara was desperate to get out and enjoy the fresh air. That afternoon, she and Gaven walked out onto the wide back patio at Winterbloom. She breathed deep, enjoying the scent of summer and the sun on her face.

Straight ahead, the owners' cabin sat tucked within a copse of trees on a small hill, and in between the cabin and the patio was a beautiful butterfly garden that Chloe herself tended. A gentle breeze tousled Clara's hair as she and Gaven walked into the yard and toward the small grove that connected with the forest farther on.

It frightened her to think she was so close to her uncle's home, that simply walking through the woods could lead her back there. But Winterbloom was a haven, and she could see why Chloe loved it so much. Having heard about Chloe's grandmother, and the fondness they shared for the house and surrounding land, Clara couldn't help but fall in love with the place herself.

In the garden, she and Gaven settled on a wooden bench.

"I'm so glad you came over," she said, unable to hide her girlish nervousness.

"I wanted to see you. Running into Lisa just gave me a good reason."

"You don't think anyone heard her, do you?" Worry knotted in her stomach.

"I don't know."

As if in answer, they heard the screen door open at the owners' cabin, and turned to see Jordan jogging across the yard. When he'd caught their attention, he waved his arm toward the house, indicating they should follow him.

Rising from her seat, Clara took Gaven's hand and the two of them headed to the front porch of the cabin.

"Hurry up, get inside!" he exclaimed, practically dragging them both into the living room. Shutting the door behind them, his actions frightened Clara, who cowered beside Gaven. "Have a seat," Jordan added as he shut the blinds.

"What's going on?" Clara gulped. A part of her knew she didn't really have to ask.

Jordan tugged his phone out of his pocket and showed her the screen, where a text message from Chloe was displayed.

Hide her NOW. Pendleton's here.

Chloe stood on the front porch with her hands on her hips, hoping she looked clueless. She pasted an expression of indifference on her face and listened as Mr. Pendleton spoke with an air of authority.

"An associate of mine was at Express Ohh's this afternoon and overheard a young girl mention that my niece was here." His tone was gruff, insistent. "If you're lying to me, you're harboring a minor."

"Mr. Pendleton, I assure you, I am not lying." She crossed her arms over her chest and leaned against the doorjamb. In her back pocket, her phone vibrated as a text message came through, but she didn't dare touch it. "I have never seen your niece. We've had a few people staying at the bed and breakfast over the last few weeks, but no teenagers. I have a business to uphold. I certainly wouldn't harbor any minors, and I resent your accusing me of such a thing."

"I am not accusing you, Mrs.... *Sheppard*, is it?"

"Yes."

"I am not accusing you, Mrs. Sheppard. I am following up on what I've heard."

"If you think she's here, then come on in." She opened the door, stepping into the foyer and spreading her arms wide. "Feel free to look around as much as you like. I promise you, there are *no* teenagers on the premises." She caught the gaze of her friend Melissa Edwards, who'd arrived only moments before Mr. Pendleton, standing in the sitting room with a cup of iced tea in her hand.

Melissa was one of the most observant people Chloe had ever known, so she knew the woman would keep her mouth shut. Chloe had already told her about Clara, and it was clear the situation was growing uncomfortable.

Harris Pendleton stepped inside, moving his bulk into the hallway where he peered toward the kitchen. Nodding a curt hello to Melissa, he took Chloe's invitation and began looking around.

"Please, feel free to look upstairs, as well," she said, not bothering to hide her irritation. "My husband and I don't have anything to hide."

"Thank you. I think I'll do that."

When he stepped upstairs and out of view, Chloe moved around the corner into the sitting room and pulled her cell phone out of her pocket. Sliding her finger across the screen to access the text message, she breathed a sigh of relief when she saw Jordan's name.

Clara and Gaven are over here. Let us know when it's safe.

She shoved the phone back in her pocket and listened to the creaking footsteps above as Mr. Pendleton snooped around Winterbloom.

"Why'd you let him up there?" Melissa asked in a hoarse whisper, brushing her long hair behind her with one hand. "Where's Clara?" She already knew the story, and had promised not to tell a soul.

"Over at my place in the back." Chloe lifted an index finger to her lips. "You don't know a thing."

"Nada," Melissa agreed, pursing her lips, as the heavy man moved back toward the steps and down to the first floor.

"I owe you an apology, Mrs. Sheppard." He extended a hand, and Chloe shook it warily. "I can see my niece is not here." He released her hand, gave her a business card, and headed for the front door. "However, if you do see Clara, please call me. I am very worried about her, and so is my wife."

Once the door had shut and the women could hear his receding footsteps on the front porch, Chloe exhaled heavily, her heart pounding her chest. "Holy crap. I guess there's a first time for everything."

"What do you mean?" Melissa asked.

Chloe cringed, her hands on her hips. "I've joined the criminal world. I'm harboring a minor!"

Chapter Thirty-One

Clara clutched her stomach. "I think I might be sick."

"It'll be okay," Jordan assured her. "Chloe just texted me that he left. She let him look around, and when he didn't find you, he gave up."

"I still feel sick."

"Just take a deep breath. It'll be fine."

Beside her, Gaven was quiet. She turned and looked at his stillness, his empty expression. He seemed troubled. "Gav?"

"I'm sorry I can't offer more comfort," he said, watching Jordan stroll from the room. "They think I can give you that, but I can't."

"Gaven, what are you talking about? Just by being here, you're giving me comfort." She sidled close to him, tucking her head against his chest. "You make me feel grounded. Just being near you…it's like I'm safer, somehow."

"But you're not. A lot of good I'd do in a crisis. I can't even get pissed properly." He shook his head in apparent disgust of himself, and her heart broke with his. It was as if they were one; he couldn't experience something without her sensing it.

Tears brimmed in her eyes as she wrapped her arm around him. He tucked her close to his body, holding her. "You're making me feel good right now," she whispered. "Touching me like this. Don't you see?"

When he said nothing, she leaned up to look at him. "Gaven, you're the reason I got away from there. *You* talked me into climbing over that wall. I wouldn't have done it without you. After we met, I couldn't get you out of my head. I wanted to be with you, and I still do. Thank you. Thank you so much for helping me out of there, for talking me into it. I'd still be there if it weren't for you."

"Clara, you're strong, stronger than you realize." With a gentle touch, he caressed her cheek, gazing into her eyes. "You could've done it without me. If—"

"No, don't say *if*. I don't want to think about that. I just want to be with you."

His brow crinkled, his eyes betraying his amazement. "How can you want me?"

She smiled through her sorrow, tears rolling down her cheeks. "How can I not?" Leaning forward, she pressed her lips against his, the saltiness of her tears mixing with the sweet taste of his kiss. "I love you, Gaven."

They held each other for a long time while Jordan busied himself on the back porch, giving them privacy. In less than a week, Clara would be eighteen, but she knew she'd still be frightened. She couldn't sleep well, couldn't dream, couldn't think without worrying Uncle Harris would hurt her.

Oh, Tammy. How am I going to get you out of there—and is it even possible?

Chapter Thirty-Two

The arguments were growing worse. It reminded Tammy of when she was little. Despite what her parents thought, she had vivid memories from when she was very small, and those recollections haunted her waking moments.

Dad wasn't too bad of a drinker these days, but he'd been worse once. Much worse.

During the nighttime visits, his breath always stank of liquor. Recently, he became too preoccupied with Clara's disappearance to bother with Tammy.

Thinking back to all the times Clara had taken her place, looked after her, Tammy grew angry. Resentful. She couldn't name her emotions, but they boiled within her, threatening to make her scream. She hid in the wall of the attic where Clara had once hidden, wishing her cousin were there with her, holding her. Why did she have to leave like that, without any word?

She remembered what Clara had said about the boy she'd met, and it was probable she was with him. Even knowing this, she kept her mouth shut and didn't say a word to her father.

The subject of Clara's age kept coming up whenever she heard her parents fighting.

Her mother's insistence he let it go—Clara was nearly an adult. Her father's fury as he shouted that he refused to let it go; he wouldn't let his brother's daughter run around without an escort—without protection.

Protection. That was a strange word to use in this house.

As Tammy hid in the attic, tucking her legs against her chest, she wondered if other girls did this. Did they hide? Was this how all families were?

She fell asleep there, her head leaning against the insulation, and waited for nightfall when her father would go to bed, and she could slink back into her bedroom like a nocturnal animal reveling in the cover of dark.

Clara folded her arms in front of her where she sat on the back patio, staring at the glass of iced tea that sat untouched on the glass top table in front of her. She looked up, watching Gaven as he wandered around in the butterfly garden, his hands in the pockets of his jeans.

Sitting at the table with her were Chloe, Jordan, and another man she'd only just met—Gioven Sparks. Chloe had suggested they might have something in common, but so far, they'd only chit-chatted about the weather, and a few of the places Gioven thought she might enjoy in Clearwater.

After a while, Gioven looked at his watch and said, "Well, I've got an appointment I have to get to." He peered across the table at Clara, his dark eyes brimming with sympathy—and something else she couldn't quite name. "Listen, I'm gonna come right out and say it. I know you've seen more than anyone your age should. But you *can* get through this, even if you think you can't." He slid a card across the table. "Call me anytime." He looked to Clara and Jordan. "You're in good hands with these two."

"Thank you," Clara mumbled, fidgeting in her chair.

"I'll see you all later." Gioven rose, running a hand down his button-up shirt, then slipped his keys out of the pocket of his jeans.

As he crossed the side yard and disappeared around the house, Clara slumped and stared at the card. "I know you guys were hoping I'd talk to him, but…I'm just not ready to talk to anyone about this…any of it." She looked up as Gaven approached. "I don't even know how I was able to tell Gaven."

The corner of his lip quirked upward. "It was meant to be, of course."

Chloe chuckled. "I think he's right. Well, I have to get some work done, but let me know if you need anything, Clara. I'm going to get dinner ready. I'll see you in the house."

Jordan rose. "Melissa was insistent on spending some time with Bianca, so I think I'm going to go relieve her. That little one can be quite the handful. See you two later."

After they'd left, Gaven pulled up a chair beside Clara. "You doing all right?"

"Yeah. Well, no. I'm not sure."

"I know. It was a stupid question."

"I'm worried about Tammy. How am I going to get her out of there?"

"You might not be able to. If she denies anything is going on…"

"Why would she?"

"Fear." Gaven's gaze met hers. "Fear is a powerful weapon."

She nodded, leaning back in her chair. A weapon like that in the hands of a man like her uncle was a horrifying combination. She only hoped her cousin would be brave. And somehow, they would both get through this.

Chapter Thirty-Three

Ryan was out doing his rounds when he got a call from the station.

"Sheriff, you'd better get back here." It was Jordan, his deputy, and he sounded anxious.

"Jordan, what's wrong? I'm just down on King Street. Heading back your way."

"Mr. Pendleton's here."

"Oh, shit." Ryan clenched his jaw as he turned onto Main. "Say no more. I'll be there in a few."

"Good." Jordan hung up, and Ryan dropped his cell phone on the passenger seat.

When he pulled up to the station, he saw a shining black BMW parked out front. Pendleton's car, most likely. He'd been expecting this ever since he reported Pendleton to Social Services a few days ago.

Here goes nothin'.

Ryan parked and slowly walked up to the building, knowing Jordan had everything under control. He couldn't have picked a better deputy.

In the station, Pendleton loomed like a dark cloud on a sunny day. Dressed in casual business attire, he paced until he spotted Ryan walking inside. He fixed him with a stony glare and snapped, "I want to speak with you. Now."

"Let's go into my office."

At first, Pendleton looked as though he might refuse. Then he stalked past Ryan and into the office, but he didn't sit down. Ryan shut the door and stepped behind his desk, his hand resting on the butt of his gun.

"How can I help you, Mr. Pendleton?"

"Cut the shit," the man growled. "I know you sent Social Services after me and my family. How dare you?"

"We received reports you've been abusing your daughter, and your niece. I had no choice."

Pendleton's fury was potent, but he gritted his teeth and spoke in a calm voice. "I am *not* a child abuser. You already know exactly what I am and what I can do." He leaned over the desk, staring directly into Ryan's eyes. "And let me tell you something, Sheriff. I won't stand by and let you destroy my reputation."

"Oh? And what will you do about it?"

He wasn't sure why he asked, because he already knew. The past was catching up to Ryan. Pendleton swore the sheriff could never touch his family, and he told him why.

He *knew*, he said. Ryan's past might've been a secret to the rest of Clearwater, but it was no mystery to Pendleton.

"You destroy me, I'll make sure you pay. You come anywhere near me, you'll lose your position as sheriff, and you'll lose the respect of this town. I'll see to it." Pendleton removed his giant ham hands from Ryan's desk and swung on his heel, storming out of the office and slamming the door behind him.

Ryan leaned forward, his head in his hands. Tears stung the back of his eyes as darkness clouded his vision. It was coming back. The nightmares, the horror of what he'd seen. Of what he'd done.

Shit.

There was nothing he could do to stop it.

Chapter Thirty-Four

That Sunday, Gaven urged Clara out of the house for a walk. He bought her a birthday lunch with the money his mother had sent him, and when they returned to Winterbloom, half of Clearwater was there. The driveway was full of cars, and when they rounded the side of the house, Clara gaped at a banner that read, *Happy Birthday!*

"Oh my God." She turned and eyed Gaven, who raised his arms in resignation.

"Hey, this wasn't my idea. I was just told to take you out before everybody got here."

All of a sudden, Chloe pointed her out, and a bunch of people turned and shouted, "Surprise!"

Rushing over to take her hand, Chloe led her to a table on the patio where a cake had been placed. Dumbfounded, Clara watched as all the candles were lit, and a number of people she'd never met before smiled and sang *Happy Birthday* in such a loving way that it both confused and overwhelmed her.

Everyone quieted down and waited. Chloe patted her on the back gently and said, "Go ahead, make a wish and blow out the candles."

Clara turned to look at Chloe, whose wide eyes were filled with affection. She looked around at all the people who surrounded her, people who looked upon her as if they'd known her their whole lives. People who seemed to genuinely care about her. It didn't make sense. Why should they care if they barely knew her?

Meeting Gaven's deep, penetrating gaze, seeing the love that resided there, she balked. This was all too much for her. Unable to stop herself, she turned and ran toward Winterbloom, her feet carrying her swiftly across the soft grass.

"Clara!" Chloe called out to her just as she opened the back door and rushed in.

Her breath was coming in short gasps, and she realized she was having a panic attack. Hurrying into the sitting room, she sat down hard and threw her head forward, sobbing uncontrollably, digging her fingers into her scalp.

Why should they care about her? What good was she? She was broken, a prisoner barely set free. She didn't feel free; she didn't feel much of anything except pain that coursed deep in her heart, a gouge in her soul she wasn't sure could ever be mended.

"Clara." Gaven sat beside her, running his hand over her back. "Calm down, breathe."

She threw herself against him, her head in his lap, and cried. He held her for a long time. She heard footsteps, someone else checking on them, but whoever it was left quickly. Maybe they knew she needed time.

"Gaven."

"Yeah, Clara?"

"I've never had a birthday party before. Why are they doing that for me?"

"Chloe likes you a lot. So does Jordan. They're trying to bring something good into your life."

She sat up, rubbing her puffy eyes.

"Do you want to try again?" he asked.

She nodded. "Yes." Standing, she placed her trembling hand in his, and together, they walked back out onto the patio.

Some people glanced at her, then looked away. The party had continued despite her running off. As before, Chloe approached her, but this time, she wrapped her arms around her, holding her close. Despite her discomfort, Clara allowed herself to lean against Chloe, to feel her warmth and the offer of friendship. It felt good, having people care about her. But it was also scary.

"You okay?" Chloe stepped back, looking into her eyes.

"No. But…maybe I will be, after a while."

Chloe brushed Clara's hair away from her eyes, smoothing it with her soft hands. "I know you'll be just fine. Now, how'd you like to blow out those candles? We'll light them again."

"Sure," she relented, tucking her arms around herself.

Gaven stood beside her while she made a wish. It was a simple wish, something most people took for granted. Something Clara wanted more than anything. Now it was up to her to make it happen.

Happiness.

Chapter Thirty-Five

He loomed over the party, easy to spot in his dark clothes.

Uncle Harris.

Clara had been eating her cake, sitting at one of the patio tables, when she saw him crossing the lawn. Even though she knew she was eighteen now, and there was nothing he could do to hurt her anymore, she still trembled where she sat. Gaven reached over and took her hand, seeming to know she needed him.

Sheriff Ryder stood nearby, having been invited to the get-together, and the look on his face was indiscernible. Something about the way he carried himself, backing away as if uncertain, made Clara think something had happened. Had he confronted her uncle?

Before she could wonder any further, Uncle Harris crossed the patio and stood before her. Some of the people at the party fell silent, causing dread to grow in the pit of Clara's stomach. How many of the guests actually knew what had happened? Humiliation forced heat into her cheeks.

Uncle Harris's gaze slid to Gaven. "Hello, and you are?"

Gaven said nothing.

When Chloe walked up, she stood behind Clara and Gaven as if to offer support. "Hello, Mr. Pendleton."

"Mrs. Sheppard." He narrowed his eyes at her. "I see my niece is staying here, after all."

"She is. But I'm afraid there's nothing you can do about it."

"You're right." His expression softened and, for a moment, he looked remorseful, saddened. He reached into his jacket and withdrew a card in a bright yellow envelope with her name on it, placing it in the middle of the table. "Happy birthday, Clara. You've grown into a beautiful young woman. I'm very proud of you, and your fortitude. I assume this is your boyfriend." He eyed Gaven again, as if wondering where they'd met. "He seems like a nice young man."

She met his gaze, and saw something in her uncle that she hadn't seen in years. He'd been damaged, too, and perhaps he wanted her to see that side of himself. "Thank you," she muttered.

"Will you be living here?"

"Yes."

Chloe placed a hand on her shoulder. "She will be staying here at Winterbloom for a little while, helping out around the house."

"Sounds like a good arrangement," he said, again surprising her with his acquiescence. "You may come to the house any time to collect your things. I'll let your aunt know, and I'm sure she'll be happy to help you pack. Tammy will be sad to see you go, but you can come over anytime and visit." He started to turn away, then added, "Your parents are proud of you, I know they are." He stared downward for a moment, as if lost in thought. "They are watching over you, always. Don't forget that."

"I won't," Clara squeaked, biting her lip to keep from crying.

"I'll see you later." Without saying another word, Uncle Harris turned and walked back the way he'd come.

Clara stared fixedly at the envelope in the middle of the table before Gaven reached out and picked it up. He moved his chair closer so she could lean her head against his shoulder. She held his hand, squeezing it tightly, hoping he would never let go.

Chapter Thirty-Six

Two weeks later

When Clara returned to Uncle Harris's house to retrieve her things, Tammy was distant and refused to talk. She wouldn't even open her bedroom door.

In the days that followed, as Clara grew more accustomed to her life at Winterbloom, she thought of Tammy often. And one day, after making a batch of cookies with Chloe, she sat at the kitchen table and stared sadly into the distance until the mug of coffee in front of grew cold.

"Clara?" Chloe sat across from her, her brow crinkling with concern.

"Yeah."

"I know you're thinking about your cousin…"

"Why hasn't anything been done?"

"Well, it's possible Tammy wouldn't talk to Social Services. But don't forget, you're close in age. She'll be eighteen soon, too, and she'll be able to leave. I couldn't offer her a room here, but there might be someone in town willing to rent to her. I'm sure she could get a job at the grocery store, or something like that."

"But why hasn't Sheriff Ryder done anything?"

"I think he's done all he can, hon. If Social Services didn't find anything they could use against him, there's nothing much that can be done right now. Just be there for Tammy, encourage her to open up. If she's as strong as you, which I've no doubt she is, she will get through this." Chloe leaned over the table, meeting Clara's gaze. "I know it doesn't sound like much, and hearing me say that probably makes you angry...I wouldn't blame you. What you've gone through is nothing you can just 'get over,' and I certainly wouldn't expect that. I'm only saying I believe in you; I believe in *both* of you even though I've never met Tammy."

"I know...I'm not angry," Clara mumbled. "Not at you, anyway."

"Why don't you go over there this afternoon and try to talk to her?"

"You think she would even listen?"

"She might. Don't try to talk her into anything. Just be there for her."

"What scares me is that Uncle Harris is *her* father, and maybe she thinks...maybe she thinks this is normal." Her eyes brimmed with tears. She was so sick of crying. "My parents were killed when I was six, but I still remember them. I still remember what it was like to be loved, really *loved*, by my mom and dad. That's part of what got me through this, part of what led me to Winterbloom. I'm not sure I would have been able to climb over that wall, and go with Gaven, if a part of me hadn't remembered Mom and Dad, and knew...*knew* in my heart that what was happening to me wasn't right."

"Clara, what you just told me shows how strong you are. Go see Tammy. Show her this part of yourself. And maybe *that* will lend her the strength she needs."

"Okay." Clara sipped her coffee, then glanced back up at Chloe. "Can I bring her some cookies?"

"Of course." She rose and grabbed some baggies out of the cabinet. "I'll pack some up for you."

"Chocolate chip is her favorite," she mused as she bit into a cookie.

She hoped the small gift would help mend things between them. She loved Tammy, and couldn't bear the thought of losing her.

Chapter Thirty-Seven

After everything she'd gone through, she wondered why she didn't just report Uncle Harris herself. Get him mired in trouble. Bury him in his own distasteful deeds.

But she knew she couldn't, not yet. Not now. She was too afraid. Having withdrawn the statement she'd made to Sheriff Ryder, she wanted to wait. There was nothing he could do to change her mind.

When Aunt Nan answered the front door, wiping her hands on her apron, she also knew she didn't want to disrupt Nan's life. She wanted to talk to her about it, but she was frightened of that, too. She wondered if Nan realized what went on in her own house, and if she did, why she didn't do anything about it. Her husband had hit her before—Clara knew this— but perhaps Nan was in denial when it came to her daughter. And her niece.

Thinking back to her birthday party, Clara recalled the pain in her uncle's eyes. She wondered what had happened to him, and his father before him, and his father's father.

She didn't know what to do, and she wasn't ready to decide. She just wanted to see Tammy.

"Clara." Nan wrapped her arms around her, heedless of the powdery flour on her apron which rubbed off on Clara's shirt.

Brushing off her clothes, Clara chuckled. It was good to see her aunt, despite the strain between them. "Hi, Aunt Nan. How are you?"

"I'm all right, dear. Been worried about you. I hear you've got a boyfriend."

"Yes…his name is Gaven."

Nan smiled conspiratorially as she slipped a pan of handmade scones into the oven. "I'm glad to hear that. Did you come to see Tammy?"

Clara nodded. "If she'll talk to me, that is. I brought her some homemade cookies."

"Well, maybe you can get through to her. She's been very withdrawn lately, I'm not sure why."

Clara bit her bottom lip, wanting to say something so badly. Wanting to ask her aunt if she realized why Tammy was so quiet, why she was *broken*. But she said nothing.

"I noticed Uncle Harris's car isn't here."

"He went out. I'm not sure when he'll be back."

Clara released a heavy breath. "I'll be upstairs, then."

"Okay, dear."

She made her way up the steps and down the hall. Knocking on Tammy's door, she found it unlocked. "Tam?" She pushed it open and walked in, but her cousin wasn't there.

Without further thought, she went to the third floor and found the door at the end of the hall that led to the attic. The hinges creaked, something Clara had once been grateful of. Whenever she'd hidden in the attic, the creaking hinges of the door acted as a warning if her uncle was coming up the steps.

Now, it was she who climbed the dusty stairs in search of her cousin. Finding a light switch, she bathed the attic in a sickly yellow glow and clambered over storage boxes, holiday decorations, and decades of Pendleton family history that sat wrapped up in ancient newspaper and moth-eaten blankets, forgotten by the passage of time.

The hiding place she and Tammy had shared was tucked away in the far wall. She climbed over boxes nimbly, quite accustomed to taking this path to reach the small passage she knew she would find on the other side of the humid room.

"Tammy…Tammy, it's me. I know you're there. I brought cookies, your favorite," Clara called out. "Uncle Harris isn't home, he went out. You're safe."

There was a slight shuffling somewhere in the dark, somewhere behind the wall, and it sounded like Tammy resituating herself.

Clara found the entryway. Like so many times before, she crouched down and clambered inside. Over the last few weeks, she'd gotten so used to living at Winterbloom, a place that afforded her both comfort and safety, that she'd almost forgotten how awkward it was crawling into this hole. How'd she done it so many times before? How'd she made herself so small in order to fit? She reminded herself it'd been out of necessity. It was probably the only place Tammy felt safe.

Questing around in the dark, once she'd entered the wall, she could no longer see. The drab light did not extend this far, and the shadows swallowed everything. But she didn't have to see; she'd memorized this path.

She knew she'd reached the corner. "Tammy?"

A harsh light invaded her retinas, and she blinked, realizing her cousin had switched on a small flashlight. Directing it away from her eyes, Tammy placed it on the floor, which was really just wood framing and insulation. By the beam of the flashlight, Clara could see Tammy had brought up a blanket and a pillow, as well as a few books. Her favorite book, *Twenty Thousand Leagues Under the Sea*, lay tucked against her chest.

"Hi, Clara," she mumbled. "What do you want?"

"I wanted to see you." She placed the bag of cookies in front of her cousin.

Tammy dragged herself up into a sitting position as Clara settled beside her, and the two girls instinctively wrapped their arms around each other. Tammy leaned her head into Clara's neck, and Clara listened to her cousin's steady breathing.

"Tammy, what'd you tell Social Services when they came?"

Tammy snapped her head up, glaring at Clara. "Nothing. You think I want to get in trouble?" She tucked herself back against her cousin. "Anyway, Dad doesn't mean to hurt me."

"Then why does he?"

"I...I don't know."

They were quiet for a long time until Clara finally said, "You know it's not normal, right? I mean...what he does, it isn't...it isn't right."

"I don't know what's wrong or right. I just know what happens to me."

"I hope you brought water up here. It's too hot in this attic, Tammy. You could get dehydrated."

"You sound like Mom."

"Does she know you come up here?"

"No. If she knew, then Dad would know."

"Just be careful, okay?"

"I will. I brought a bottle of water up with me. Anyway, it'll be freezing up here in the winter."

"I know. That's not good, either."

"Where else am I supposed to go?"

"I don't know." Clara squeezed Tammy tightly against her. "You'll be eighteen soon, Tammy. You can get out of here, too."

"With what money?"

"Chloe, the woman who owns Winterbloom Bed and Breakfast, says she might be able to help you get a job, find a place to live."

"Really?" Tammy sounded almost hopeful for a moment. "But that's not for another two months."

"I know, but it's something to look forward to. We can start planning in the meantime."

"Maybe."

They were quiet for a long time. Then Clara asked, "Tammy, do you hate me?"

"No. But…why did you leave me here?"

"I had to."

Tammy tugged herself away, crossing her arms over her chest. "You didn't have to leave me here. You could've taken me with you."

"I *asked* if you wanted to come out and meet Gaven. You said no."

"That's not what I mean!" she snapped. "Whatever."

"I love you, Tammy. I want you to be happy; I want us both to be happy. I had to leave. You have to leave, too."

"But I can't yet." Tammy glared at her, her entire mood changing in an instant. "Just leave me alone. Dad will be home soon, and if you don't go, he'll hear us talking up here. I don't want him to find out about my hiding spot."

"Okay," Clara relented. She ran her fingers through Tammy's hair and kissed her on the forehead. "I love you, cousin."

"I love you, too."

"I'll see you soon."

And with that, she climbed out of the hole and back into the yellow glow of the attic as the flashlight clicked off behind her. Tammy sank back into the dark world she inhabited, and Clara forged into the light.

Chapter Thirty-Eight

She giggled as Melissa recounted one of the real-life stories that had inspired her to write one of her novels, and they both watched as Chloe placed another plate of cookies on the table.

"If we're not careful, we're all going to gain twenty pounds eating these cookies," Melissa joked.

"I'm not worried about it," Clara said as she grabbed another. After two bites, she groaned, clutching her stomach. "Ugh, on second thought…maybe I *should* worry."

"Aww." Chloe patted her on the back, looking across the table to wink at Gaven. "Why don't you and your young man go relax in the sitting room? Stay away from the kitchen and my baked goods for a while."

"That sounds like a plan," Clara said, standing. Gaven rose with her, remaining silent, and the two of them walked into the other room.

If it were anyone else, she would've taken his silence as a bad sign. But she knew Gaven was a quiet person, withdrawn and introspective, so she wasn't concerned. She tugged him down onto the couch with her and cuddled against him. He held her close, and they fit together just right.

"It's getting late," she muttered, yawning. The sun had long since set.

"I don't care," Gaven said. "I want to stay with you. I just wish I had a beer."

"Why?"

"I'm not good at affection. I need something to loosen me up."

Clara straightened, caressing his cheek and running her fingers through his hair. "You know what?"

"What?"

"I think you're capable of more than you give yourself credit for. Anything you do when you're drinking, you can do when you're sober. You don't need the alcohol."

"Maybe."

"For example, if you were drinking right now, would you be more inclined to kiss me?"

"Well, yes."

"And you aren't inclined to do it now?" she prodded.

"I would like to kiss you. But…as I said, I am not very good at initiating affection."

"Then, allow me." Clara leaned into him, kissing him gently. She brushed her lips against his, enjoying the sensation. She deepened the kiss, encouraging him to find the passion she knew was there.

The night wore on as they held each other, and he seemed to grow more comfortable in her embrace.

A lot had changed in the few weeks since Clara had left her uncle's home. Chloe had helped her enroll at Clearwater School, and she would finish the last of her high school education once autumn arrived. She planned on calling Gioven Sparks tomorrow; she wanted to talk to him.

The horrors of her past caused insomnia, and she knew he might be able to offer some guidance. Jordan could, too. Clara was opening up in ways she never thought possible.

And it was all thanks to Gaven. If he hadn't coaxed her over the ivy wall, she never would've gotten this far this fast. Standing, she took his hand and led him across the sitting room and toward the stairs.

"Where are we going?" he asked.

"Upstairs. If you're going to stay, you'll stay with me." She turned and slipped effortlessly into his embrace, kissing him again. "I just want you to hold me all night," she whispered.

"I think I can do that."

"Promise?"

"I promise."

"I love you so much, Gaven."

He kissed her on the forehead, unable to hide his elation. "I love you, Clara."

She took his hand again and led up him the stairs. Finally, something felt right. Not only right, but wonderful.

There was no turning back. From now on, she would only go forward. And somehow, she would persevere.

Rosa Sophia

Rosa Sophia is a novelist and full-time editorial consultant. With a degree in Automotive Technology, she adores writing and editing as well as fixing cars. Rosa is also a crazy cat lady in training, and currently divides her time between South Florida and Pennsylvania.